Wow, Archie, you're a very talented fox.
So are you, Reddie!

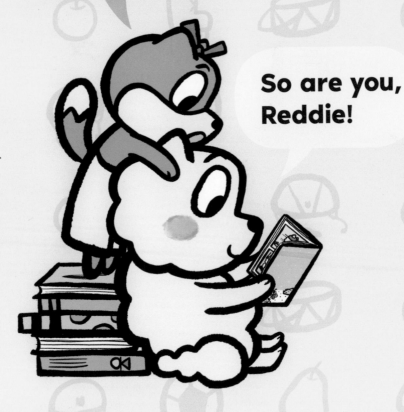

For Poppy Periwinkle,
our greatest inspiration!

Special thanks to
Chris Hernandez.

RAZORBILL

An imprint of Penguin Random House LLC, New York

First published in the United States of America by Razorbill, an imprint of Penguin Random House LLC, 2022

Copyright © 2022 by Candy Robertson and Nicholas James Robertson

Visit us online at penguinrandomhouse.com.

Library of Congress Cataloging-in-Publication Data
Names: Robertson, Nicholas James, author, illustrator.
Title: Look what we can do! : a competition! / pictures and words by Candy James.
Description: New York : Razorbill, 2022. | Series: Archie & Reddie ; book 3
| Audience: Ages 4-8 years | Summary: Fox friends Archie and Reddie are excited about entering a talent show so they practice all their moves in the hopes of winning a wagon for all their books.
Identifiers: LCCN 2021035094 | ISBN 9780593350164 (hardcover) | ISBN 9780593350195 (ebook) |
ISBN 9780593350171 (ebook) Subjects: CYAC: Graphic novels. | Foxes–Fiction. |
Talent shows–Fiction. | Humorous stories. | LCGFT: Funny animal comics.
Classification: LCC PZ7.7.R6325 Lo 2022 | DDC 741.5/994–dc23
LC record available at https://lccn.loc.gov/2021035094

Manufactured in China

1 3 5 7 9 10 8 6 4 2

TOPL

Book design by Candy James. Text set in Noir Pro.

AN ARCHIE & REDDIE BOOK

LOOK WHAT WE CAN DO!

A COMPETITION!

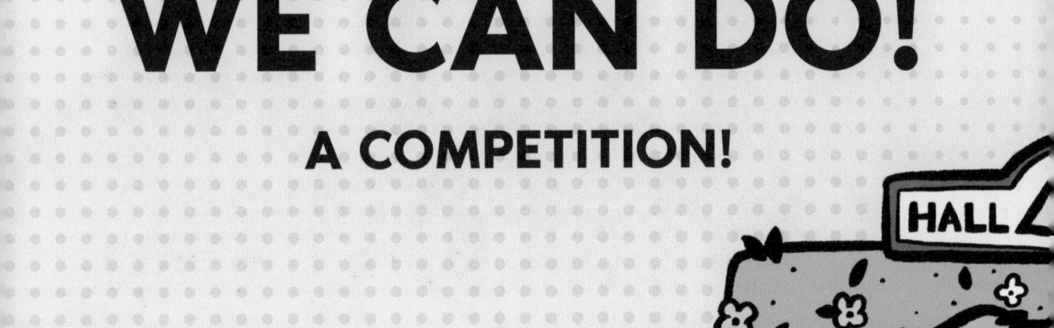
HALL
TALENT SHOW
WIN
TONIGHT

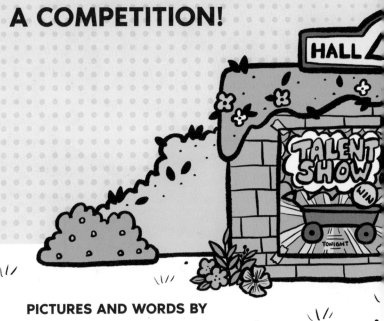

PICTURES AND WORDS BY

CANDY JAMES

RAZORBILL

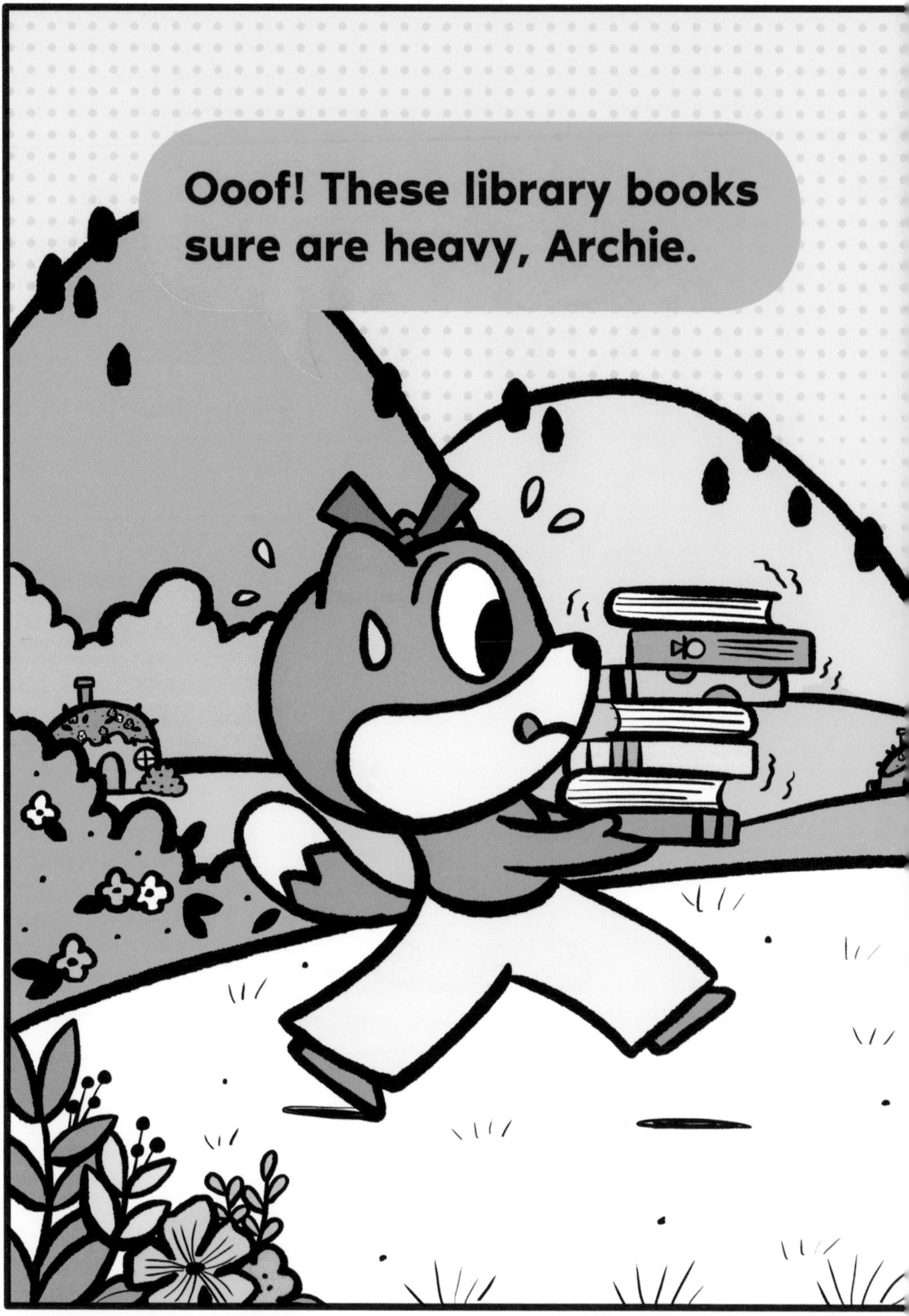
Ooof! These library books sure are heavy, Archie.

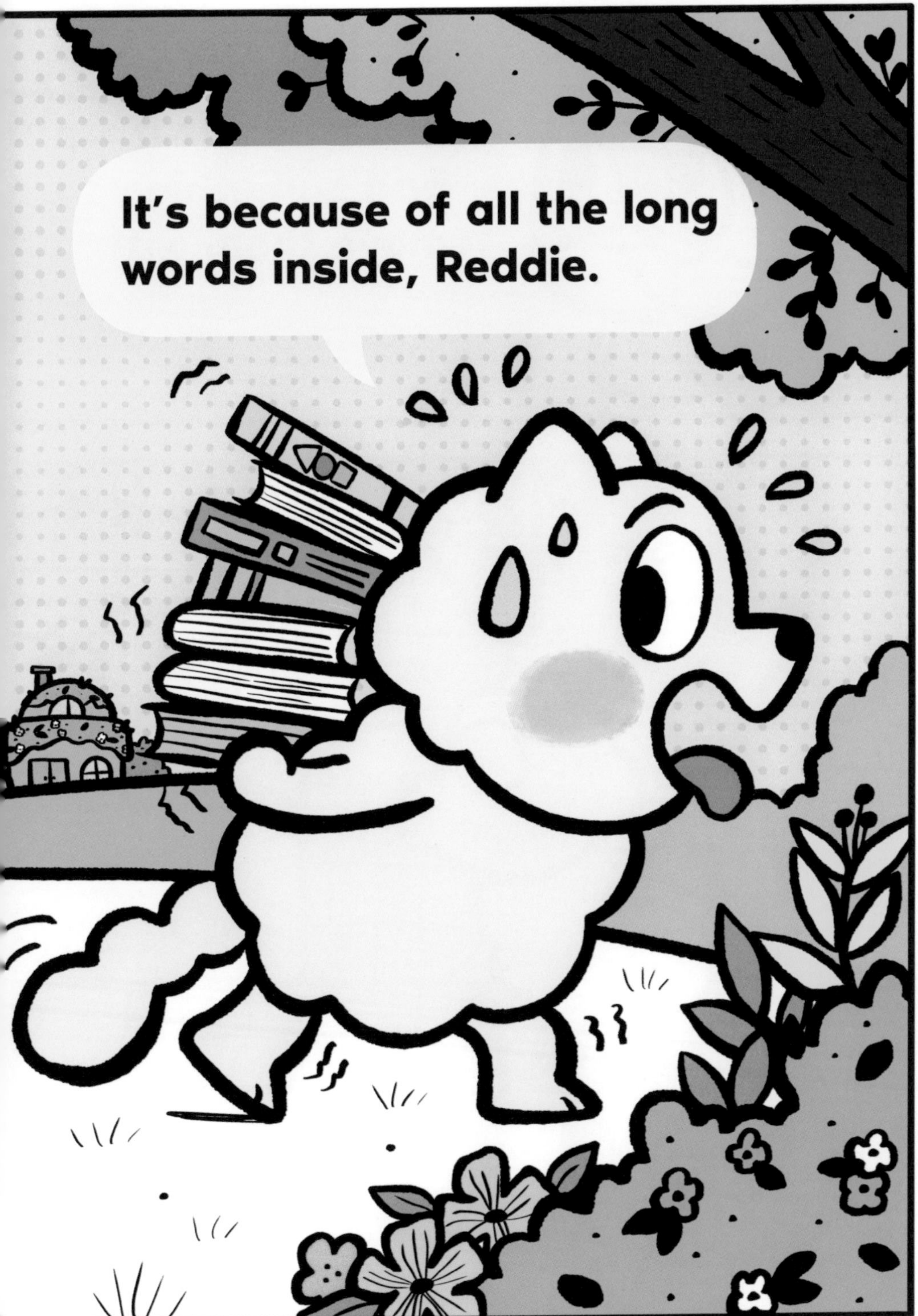
It's because of all the long words inside, Reddie.

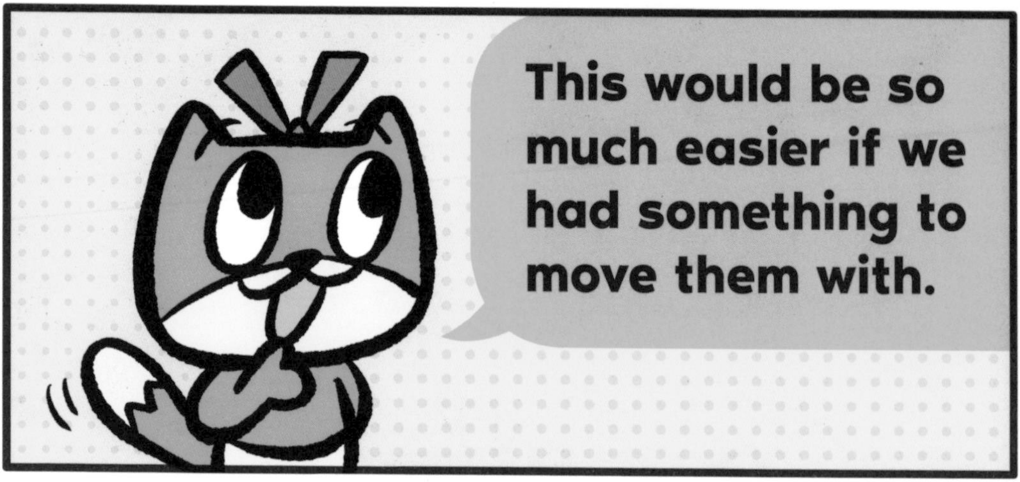
This would be so much easier if we had something to move them with.

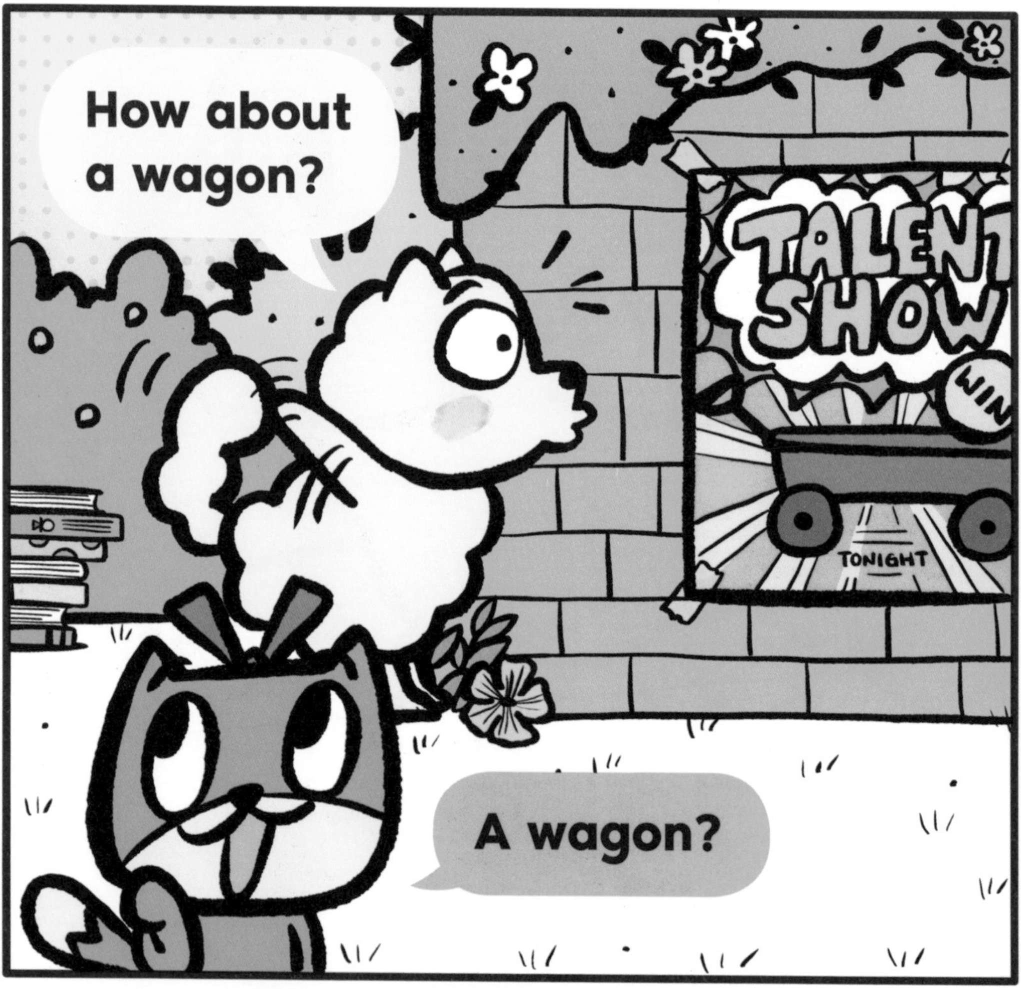
How about a wagon?
TALENT SHOW
WIN
TONIGHT
A wagon?

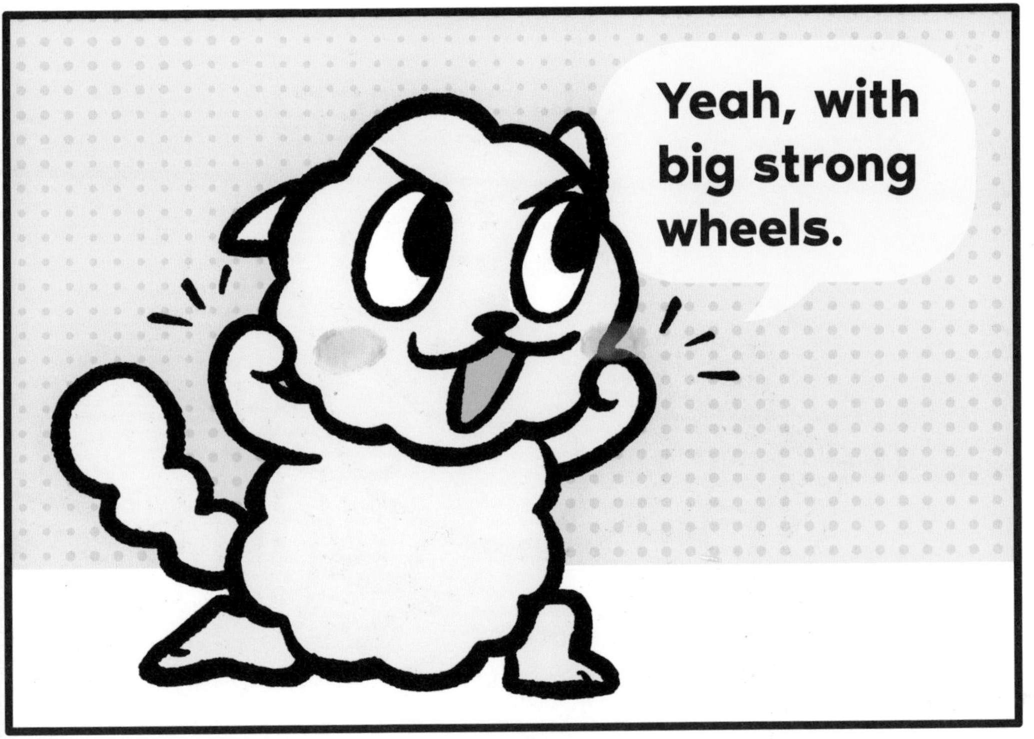
Yeah, with big strong wheels.

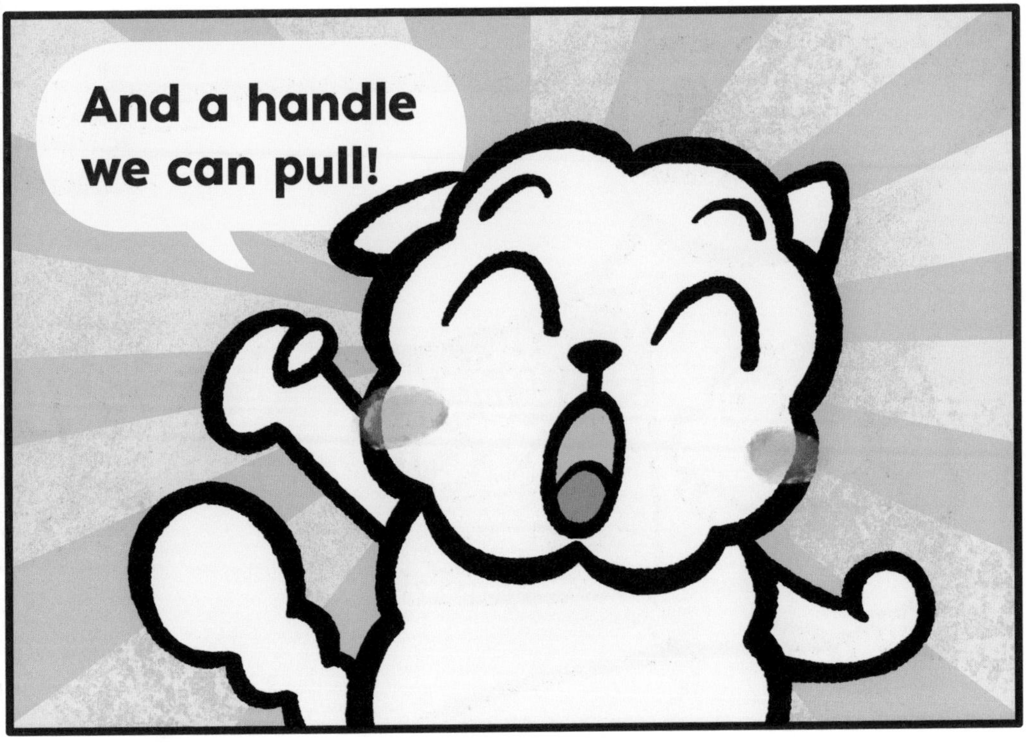
And a handle we can pull!

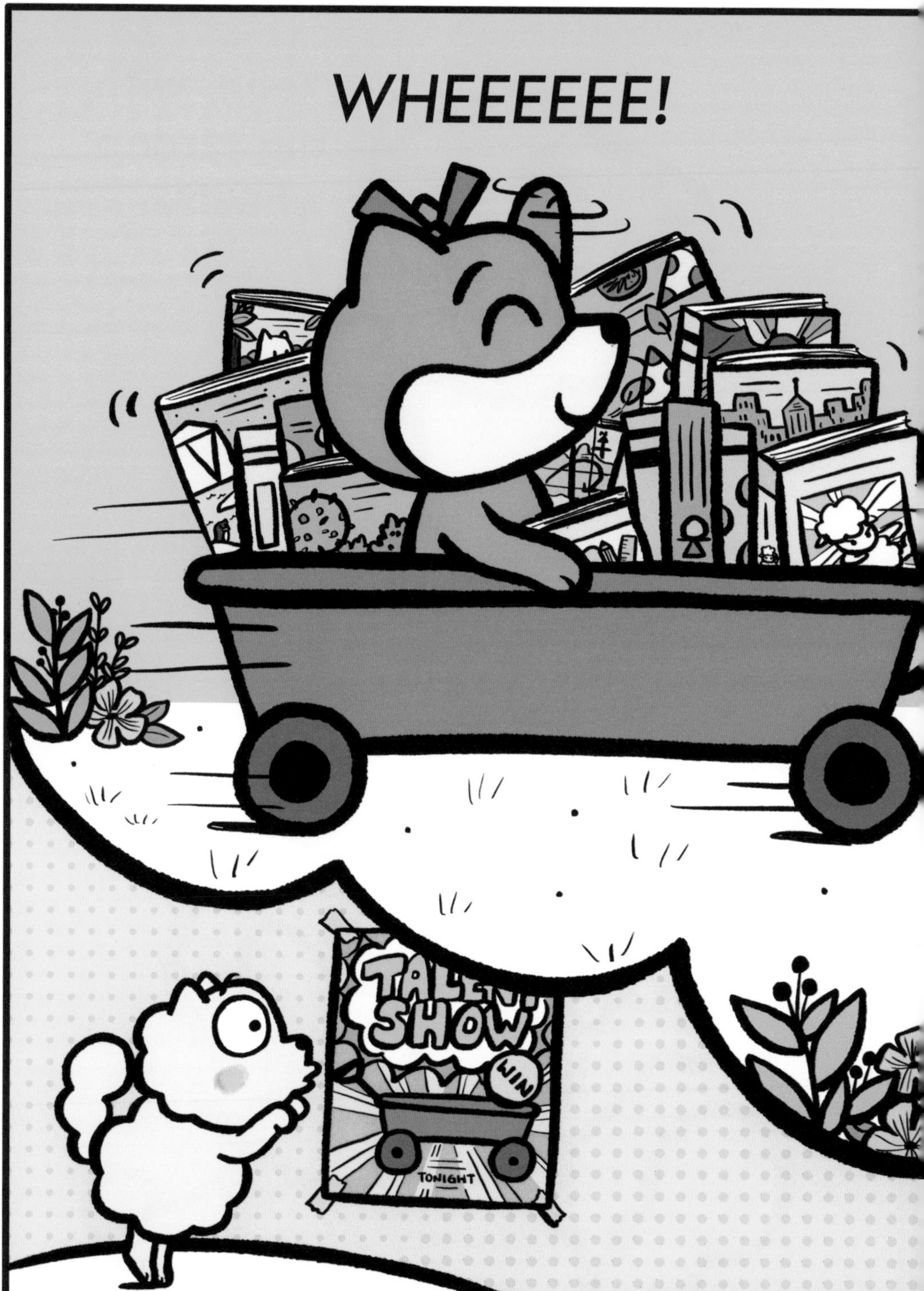
WHEEEEEEE!
SHOW
WIN
TONIGHT

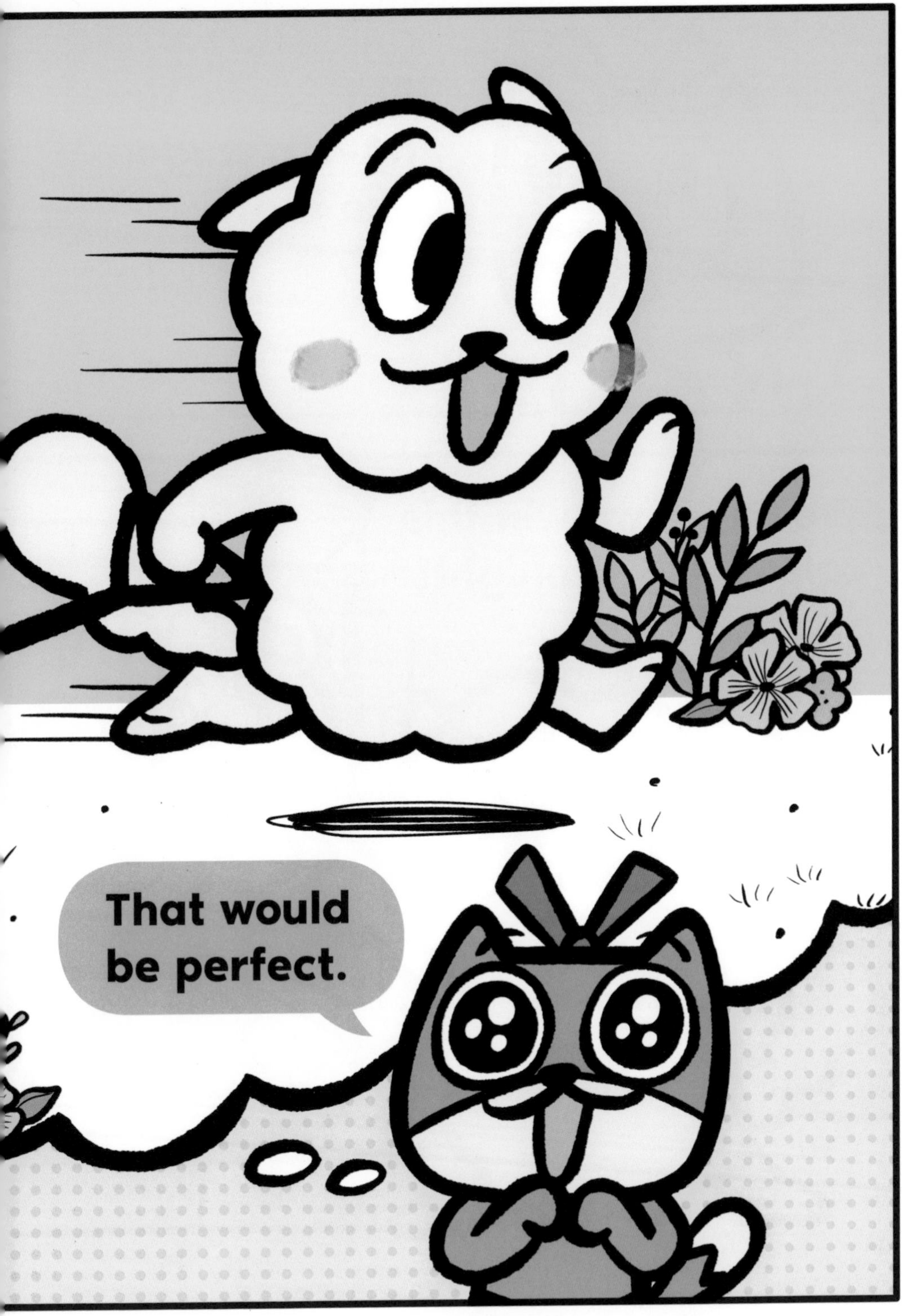
That would be perfect.

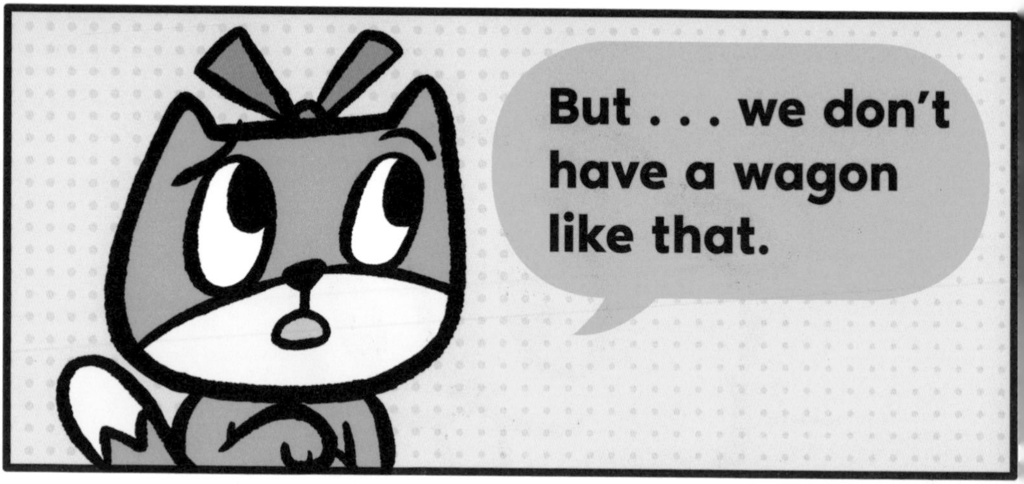
But . . . we don't have a wagon like that.

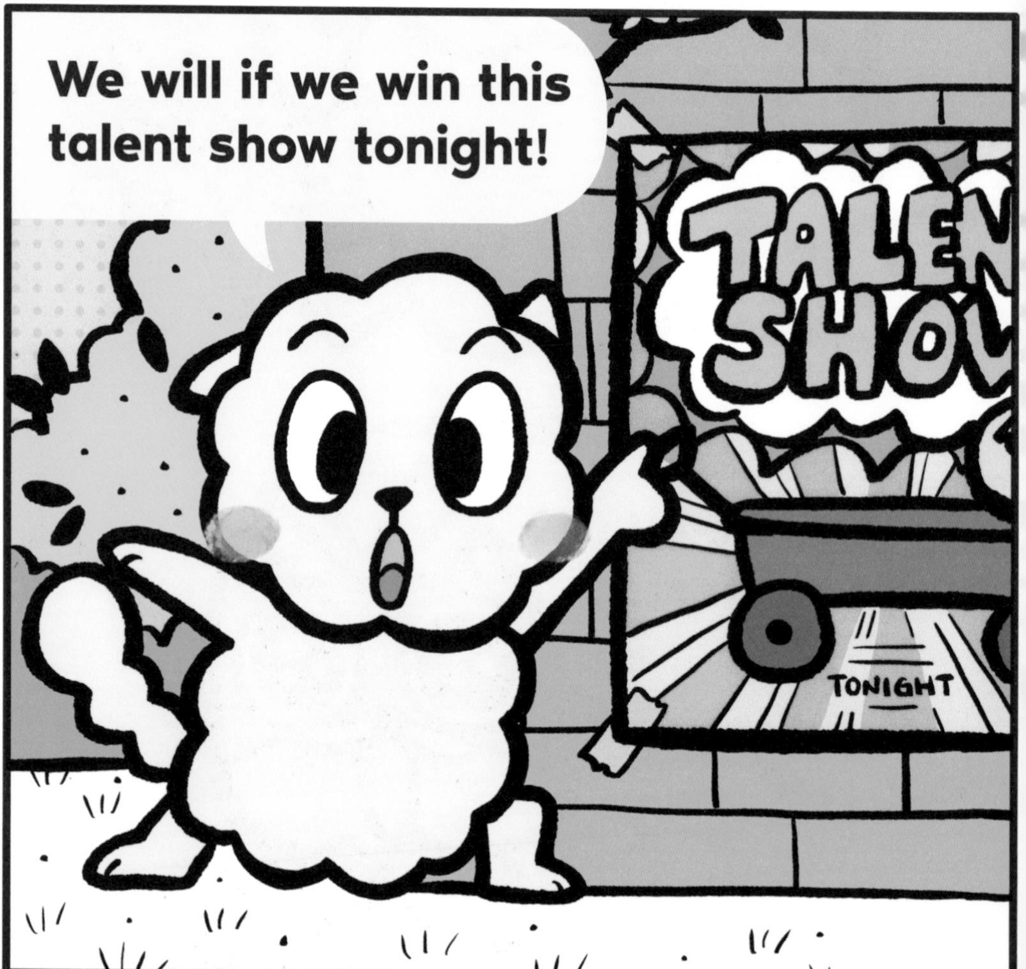
We will if we win this talent show tonight!
TONIGHT

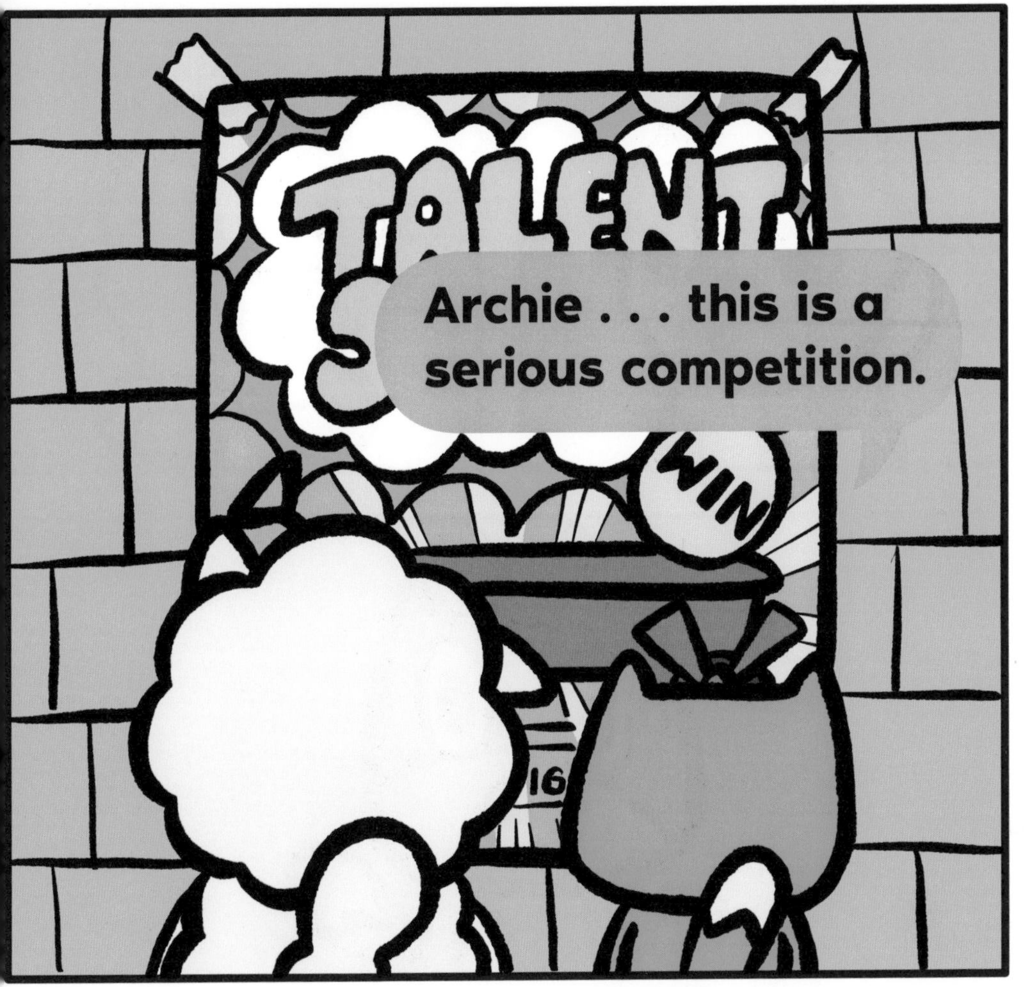
TALENT
WIN
16
Archie . . . this is a serious competition.

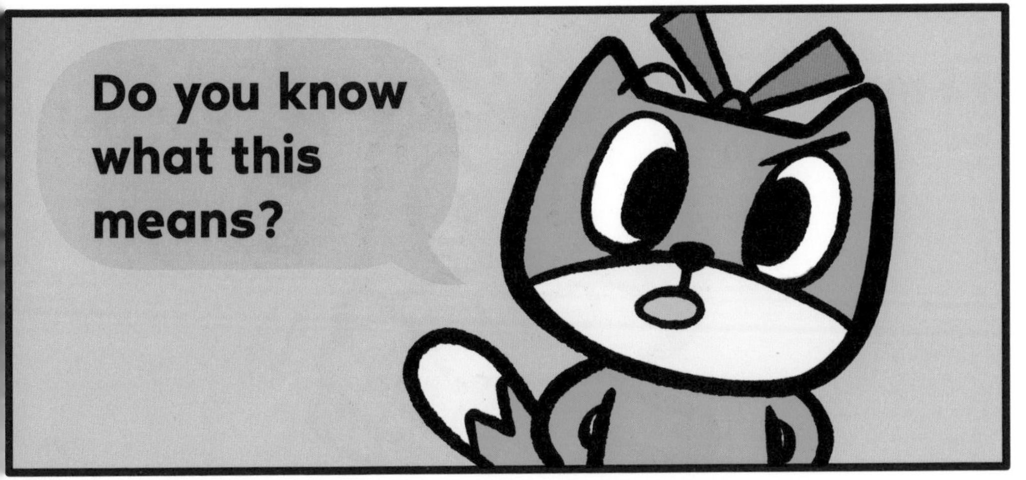
Do you know what this means?

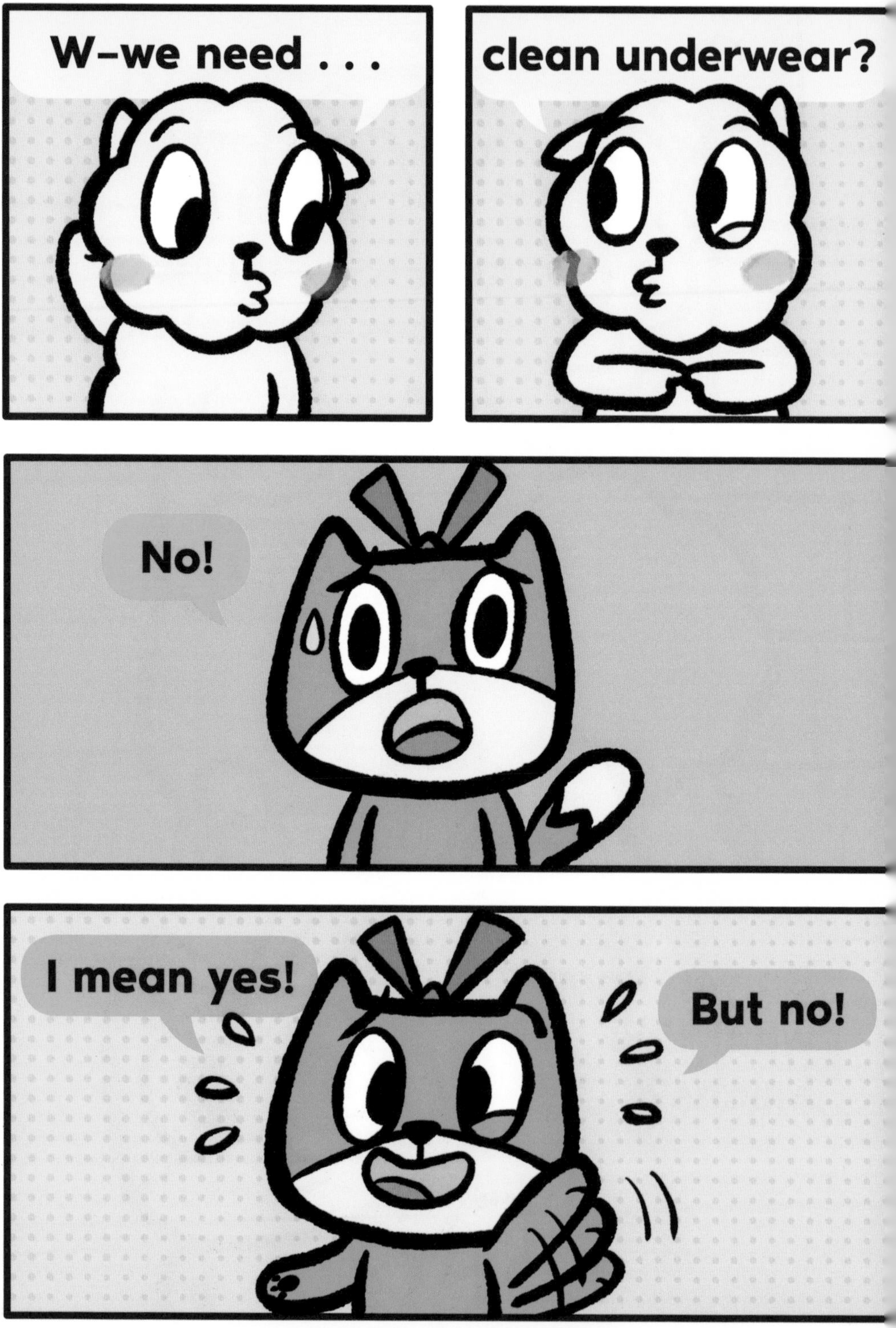
W–we need . . .
clean underwear?
No!
I mean yes!
But no!

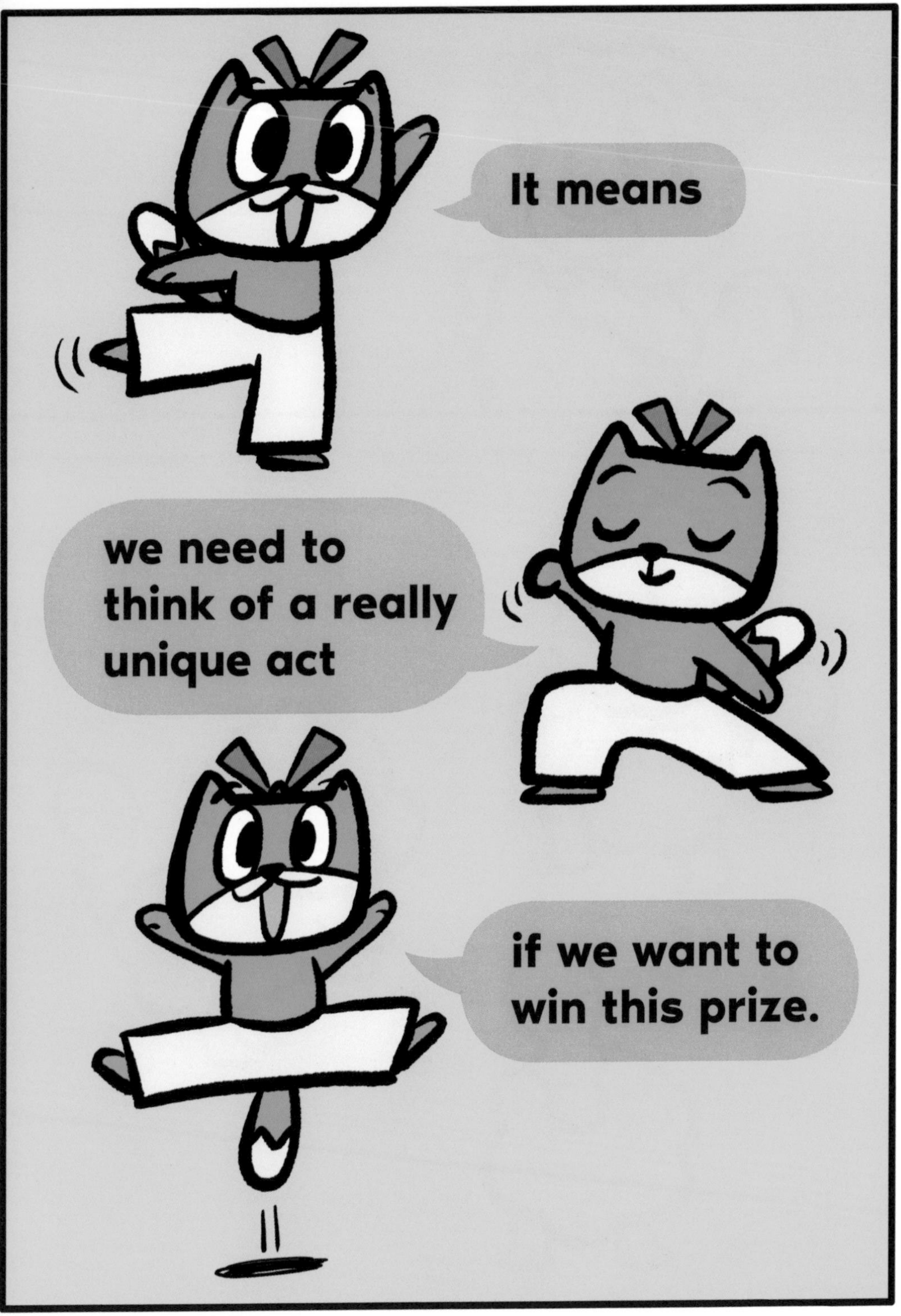
It means
we need to think of a really unique act
if we want to win this prize.

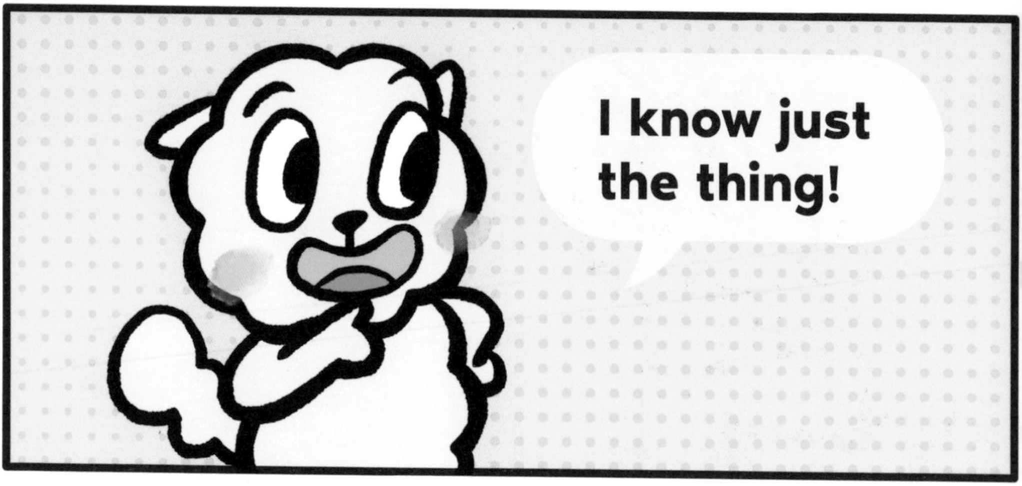
I know just the thing!

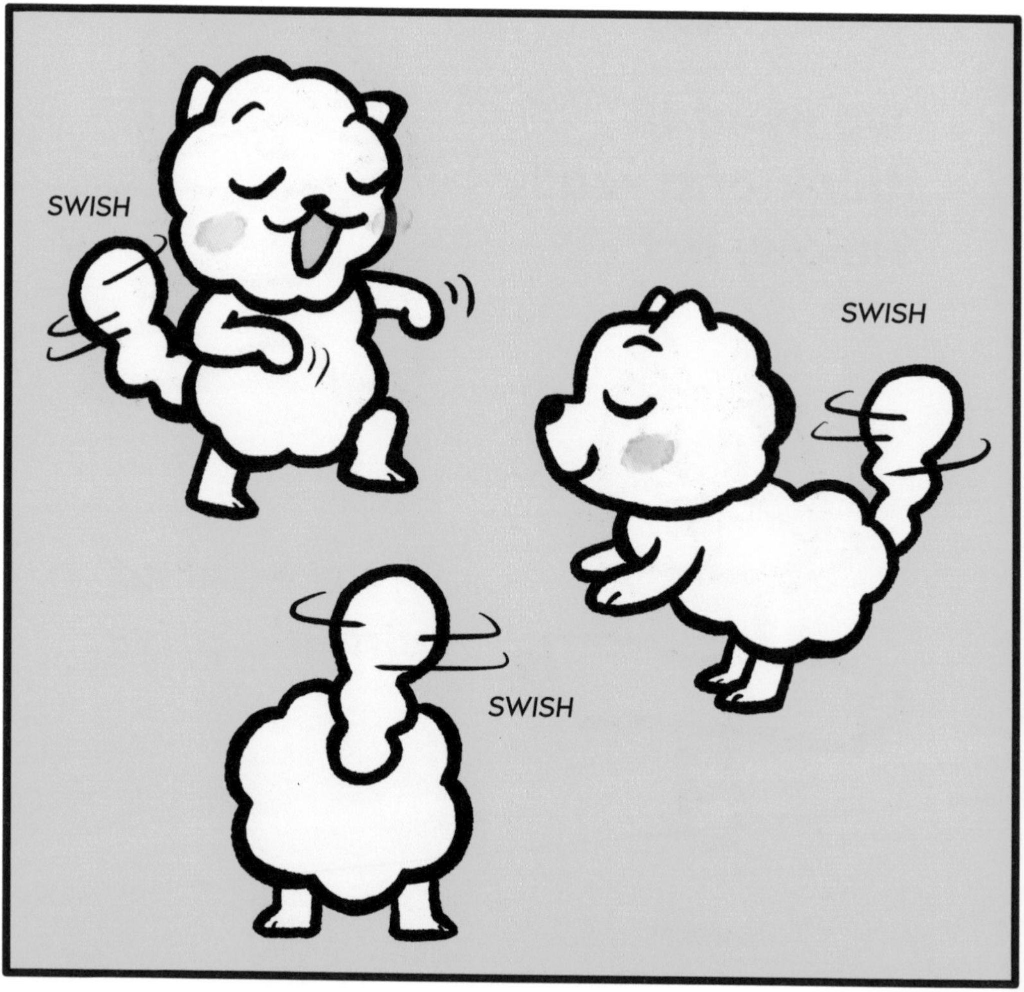
SWISH
SWISH
SWISH

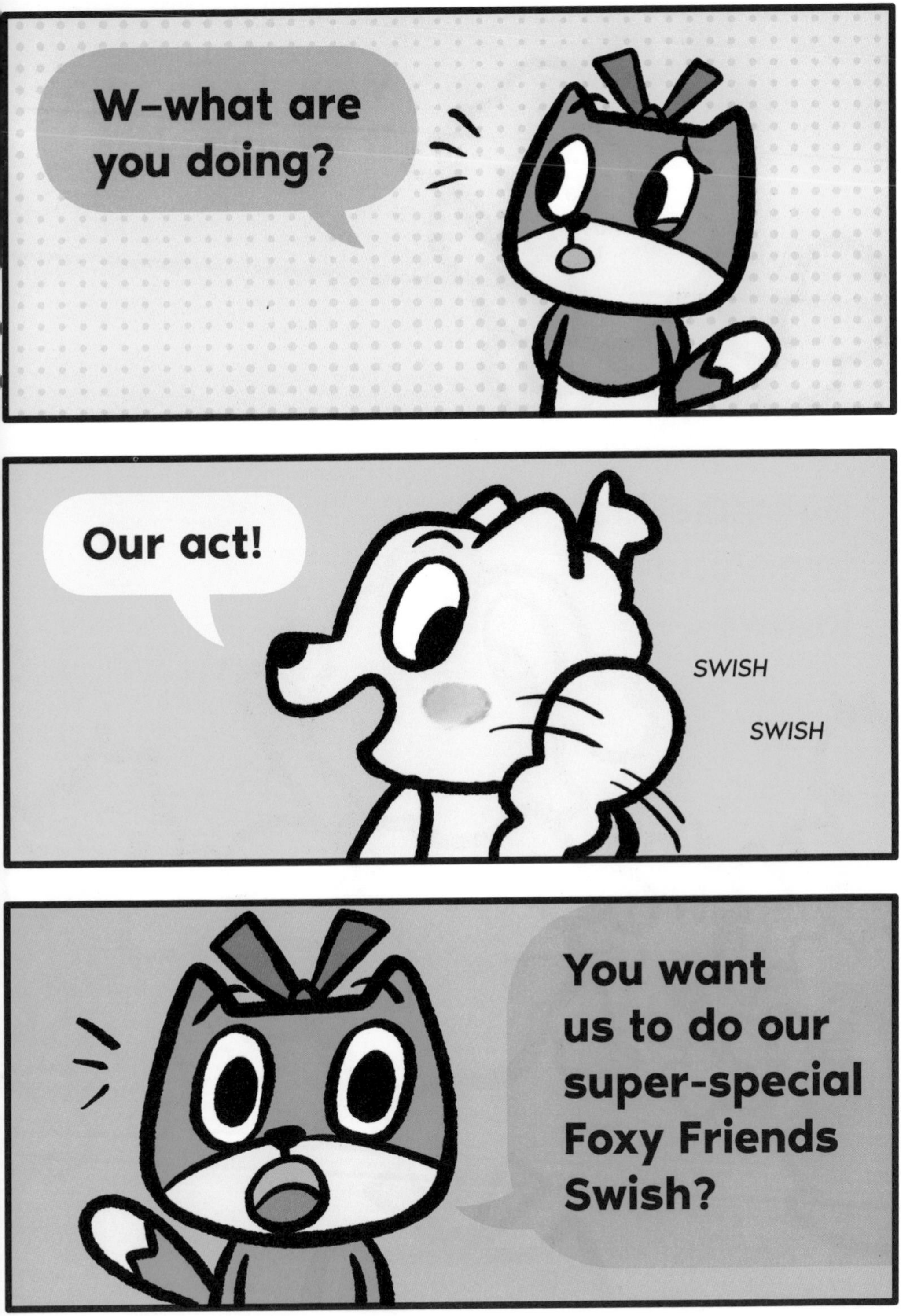
W–what are you doing?
Our act!
SWISH
SWISH
You want us to do our super-special Foxy Friends Swish?

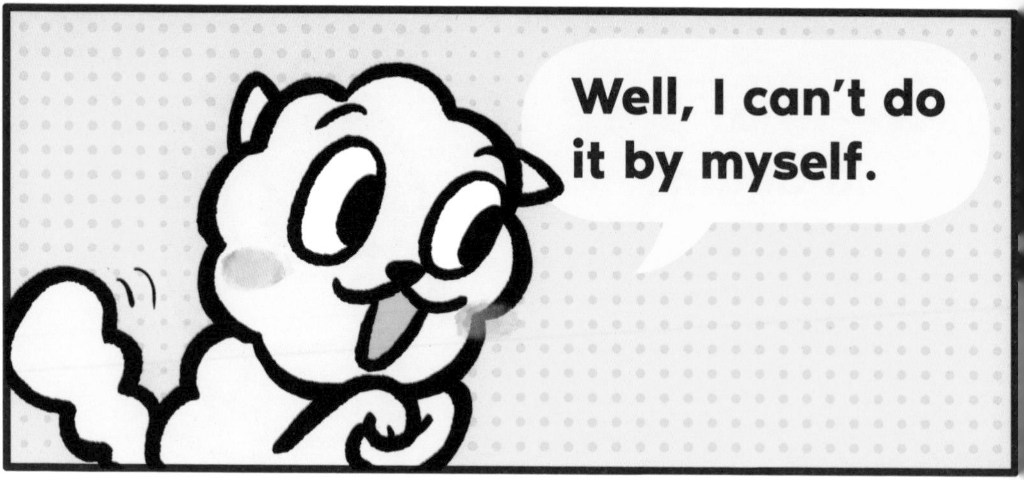
Well, I can't do it by myself.

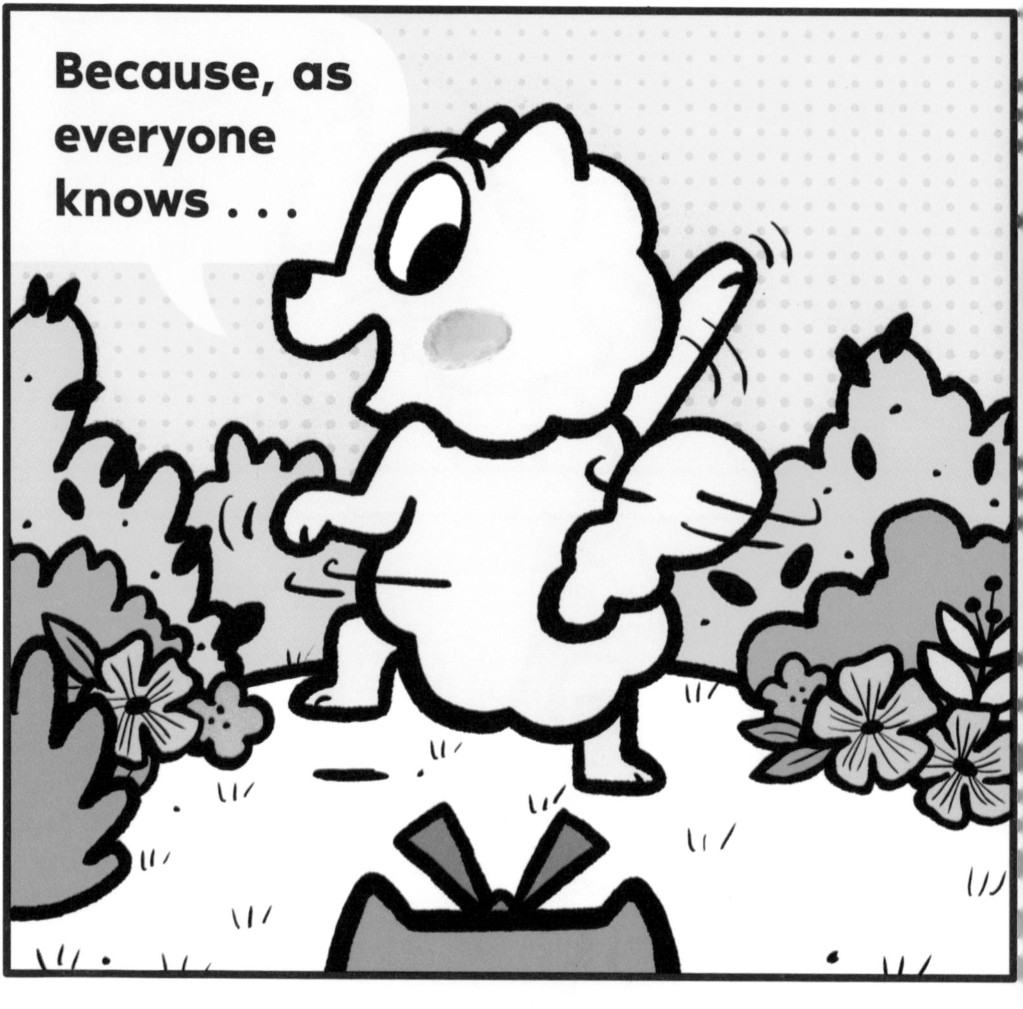
Because, as everyone knows . . .

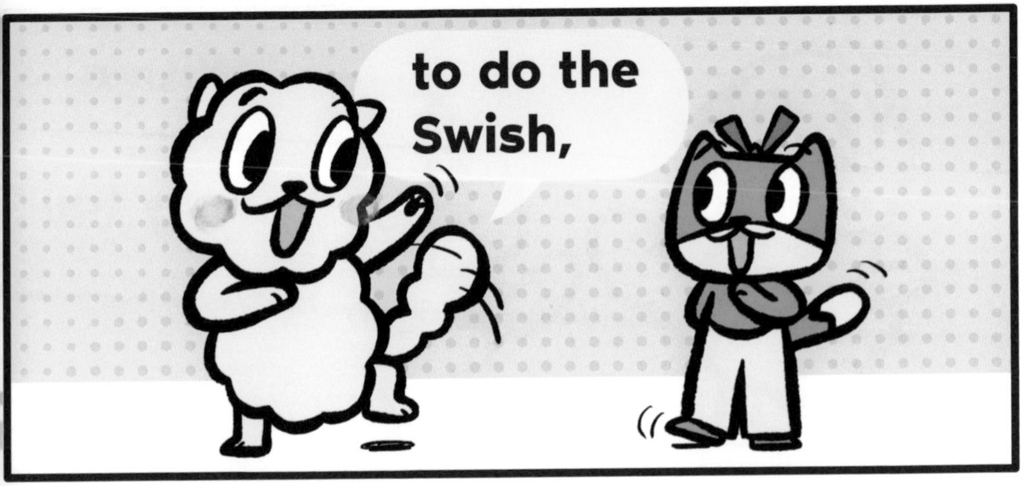
to do the Swish,

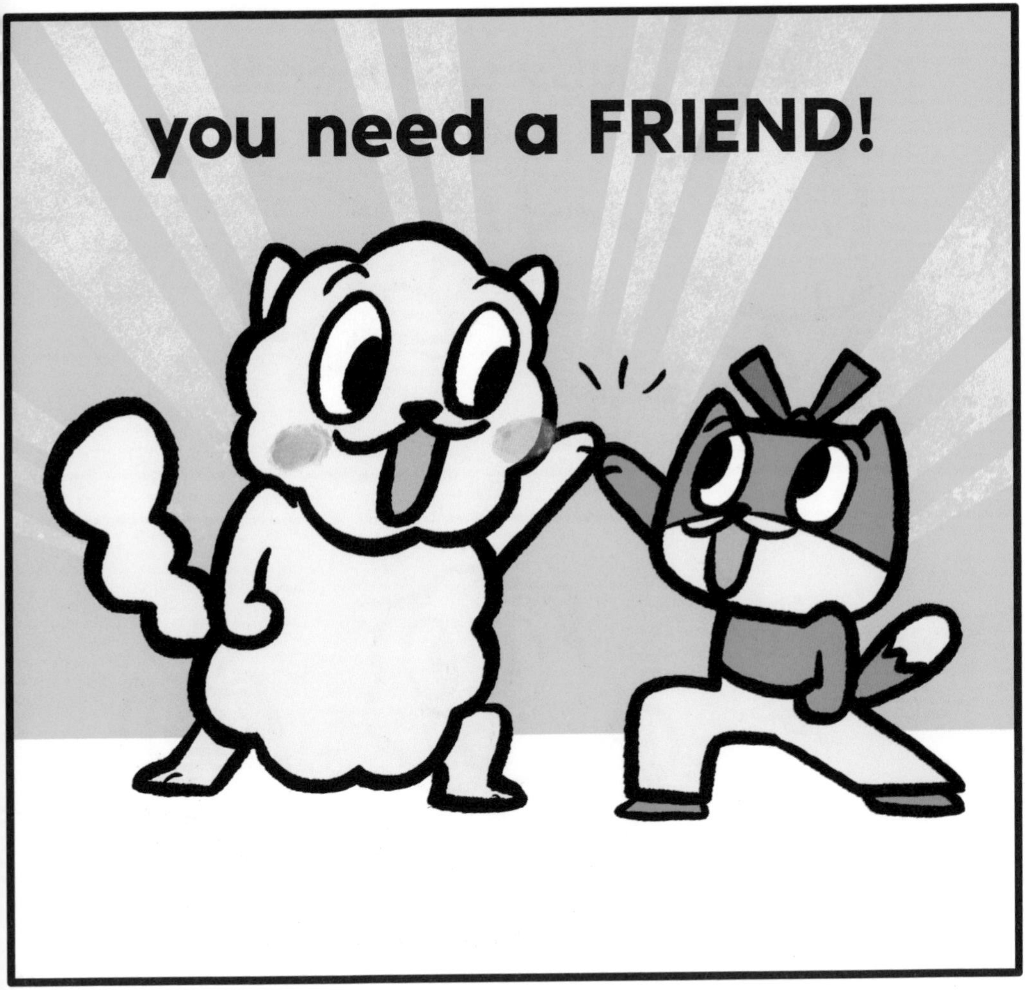
you need a FRIEND!

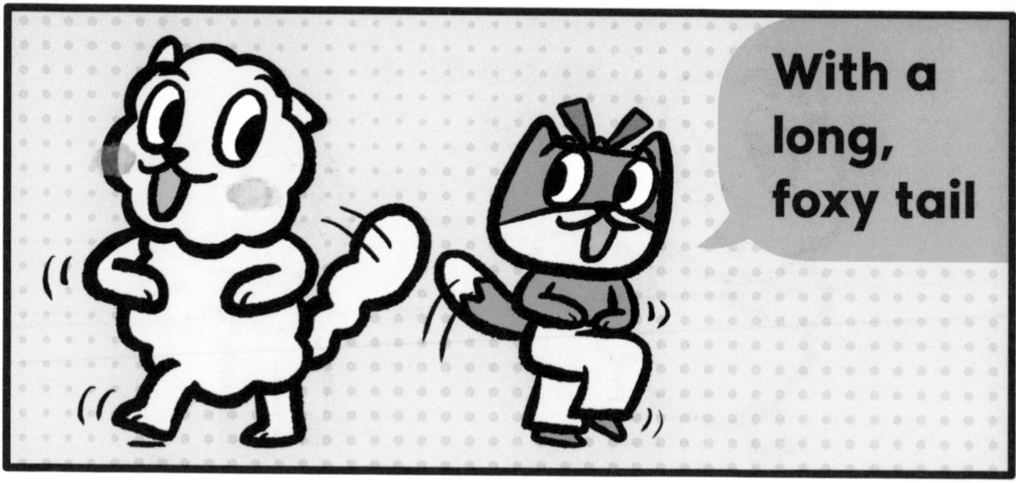
With a long, foxy tail

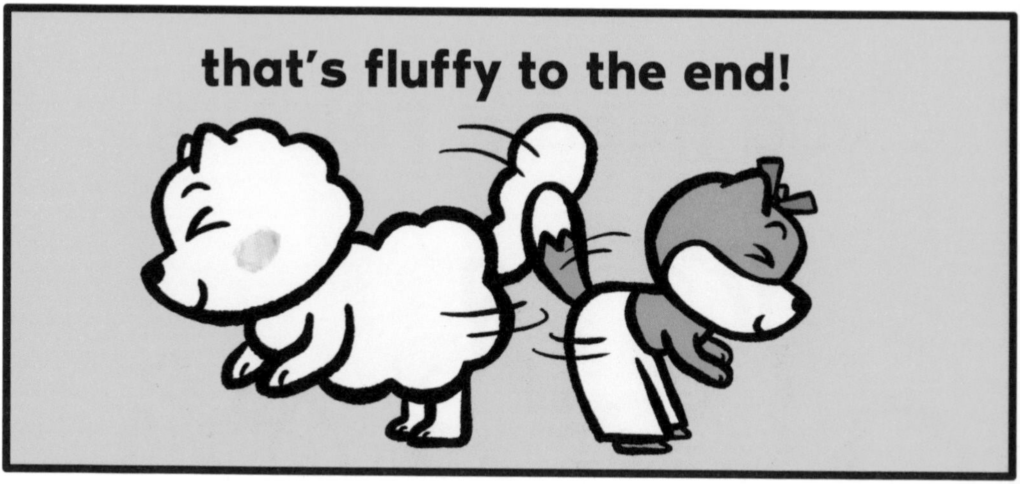
that's fluffy to the end!

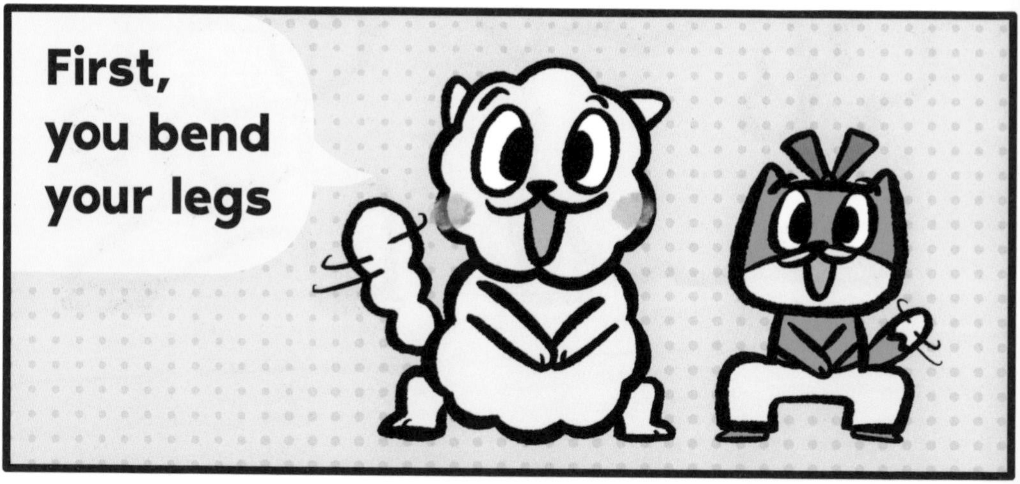
First, you bend your legs

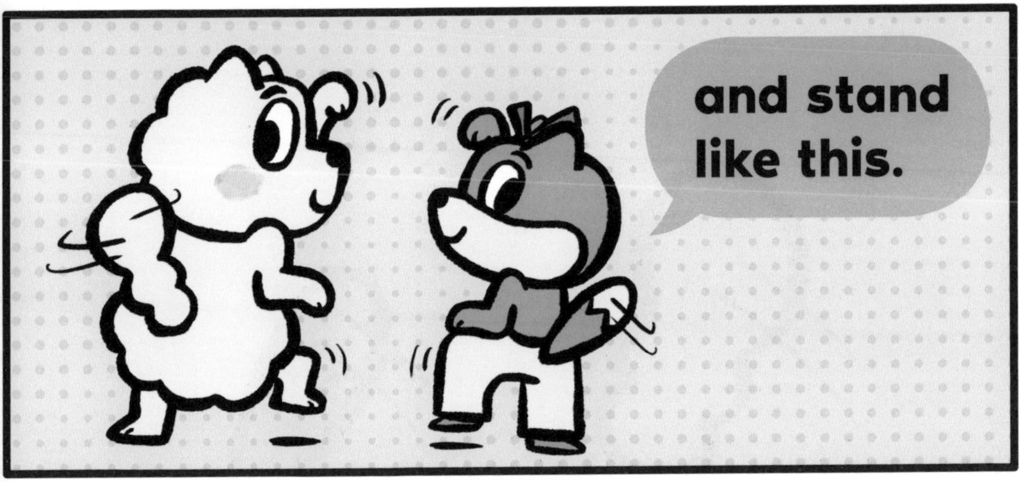
and stand like this.

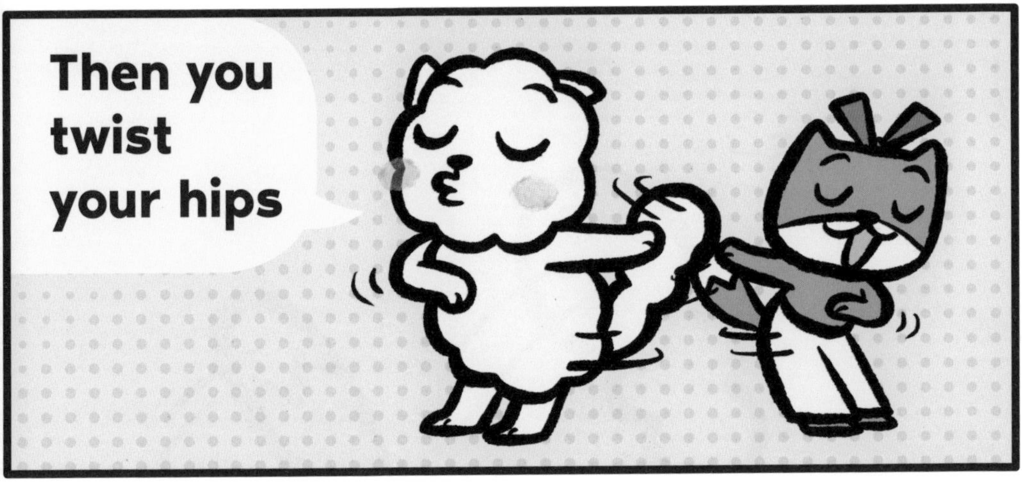
Then you twist your hips

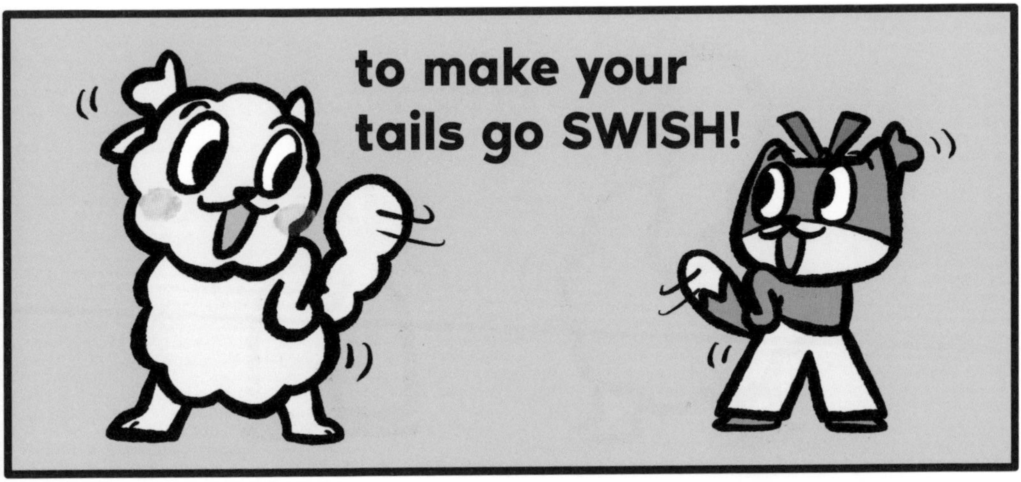
to make your tails go SWISH!

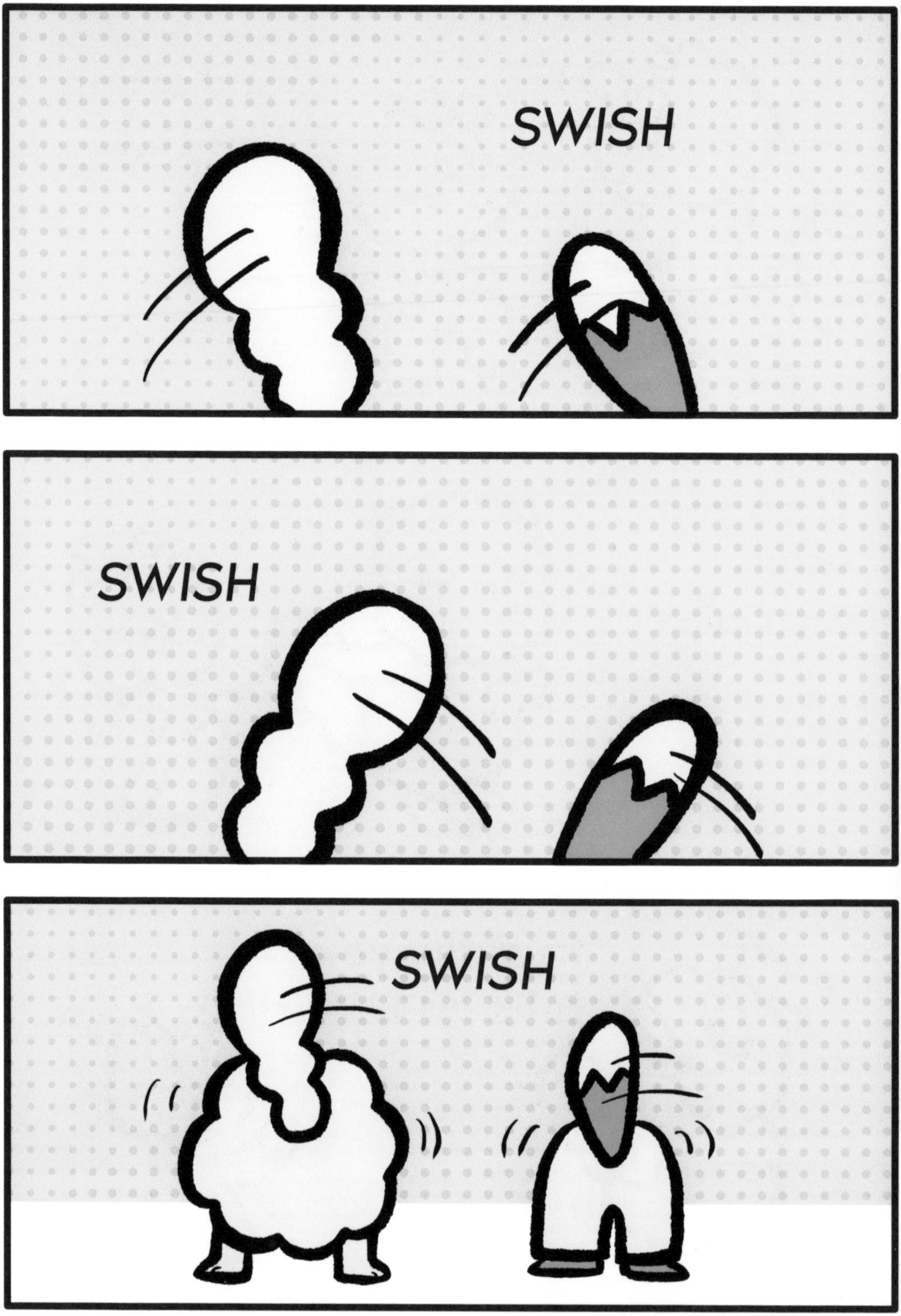
SWISH
SWISH
SWISH

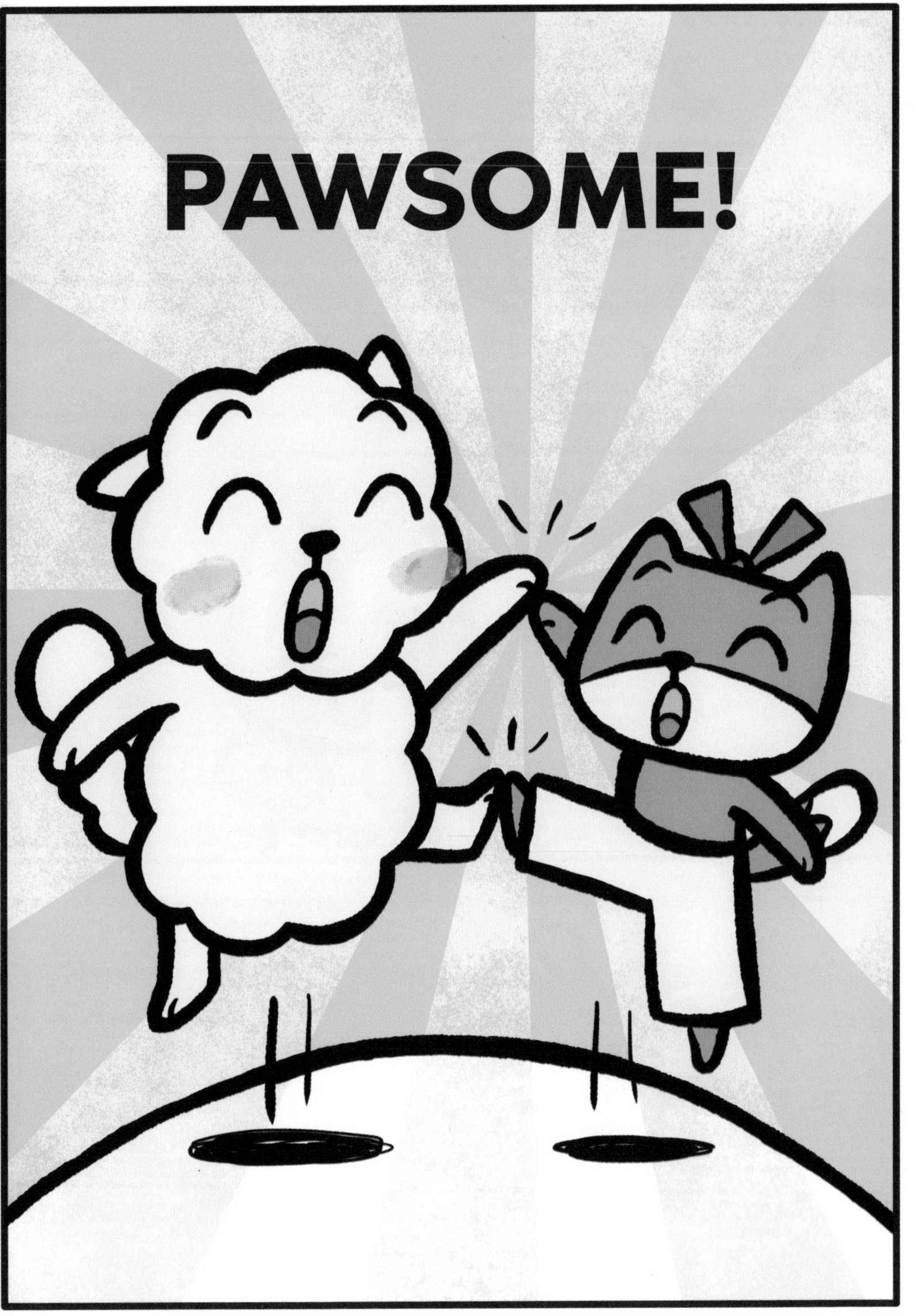
PAWSOME!

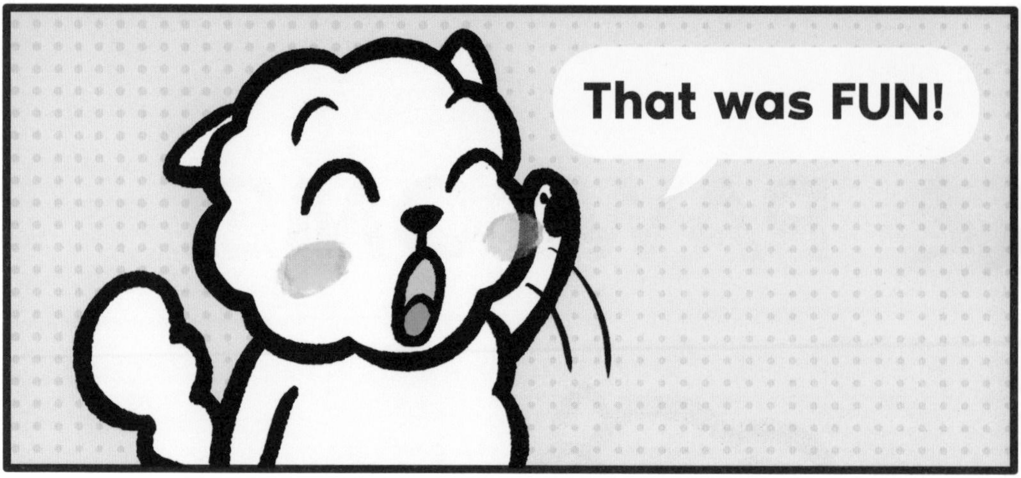
That was FUN!

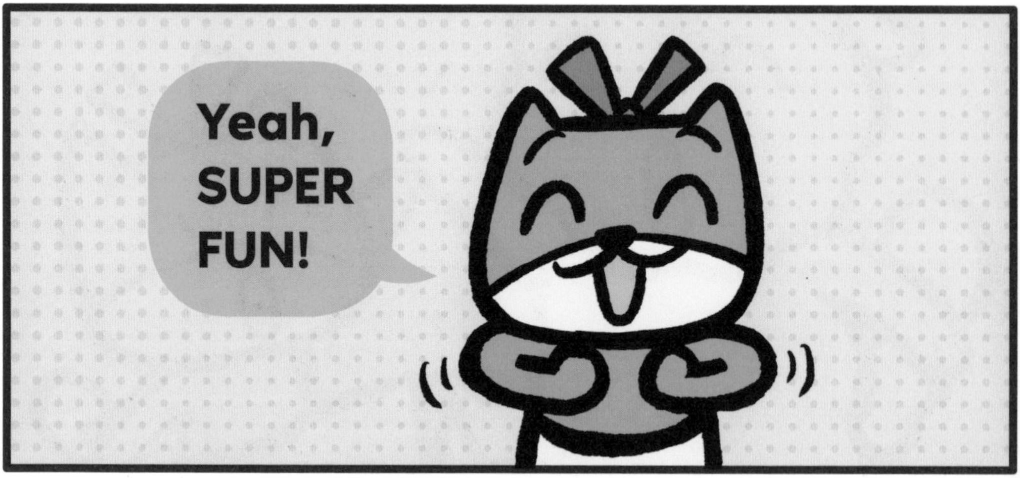
Yeah, SUPER FUN!

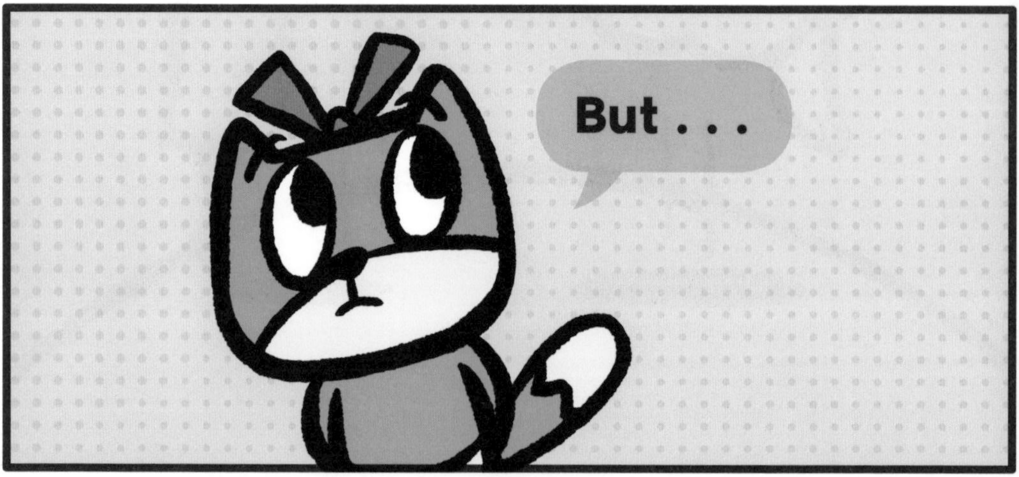
But . . .

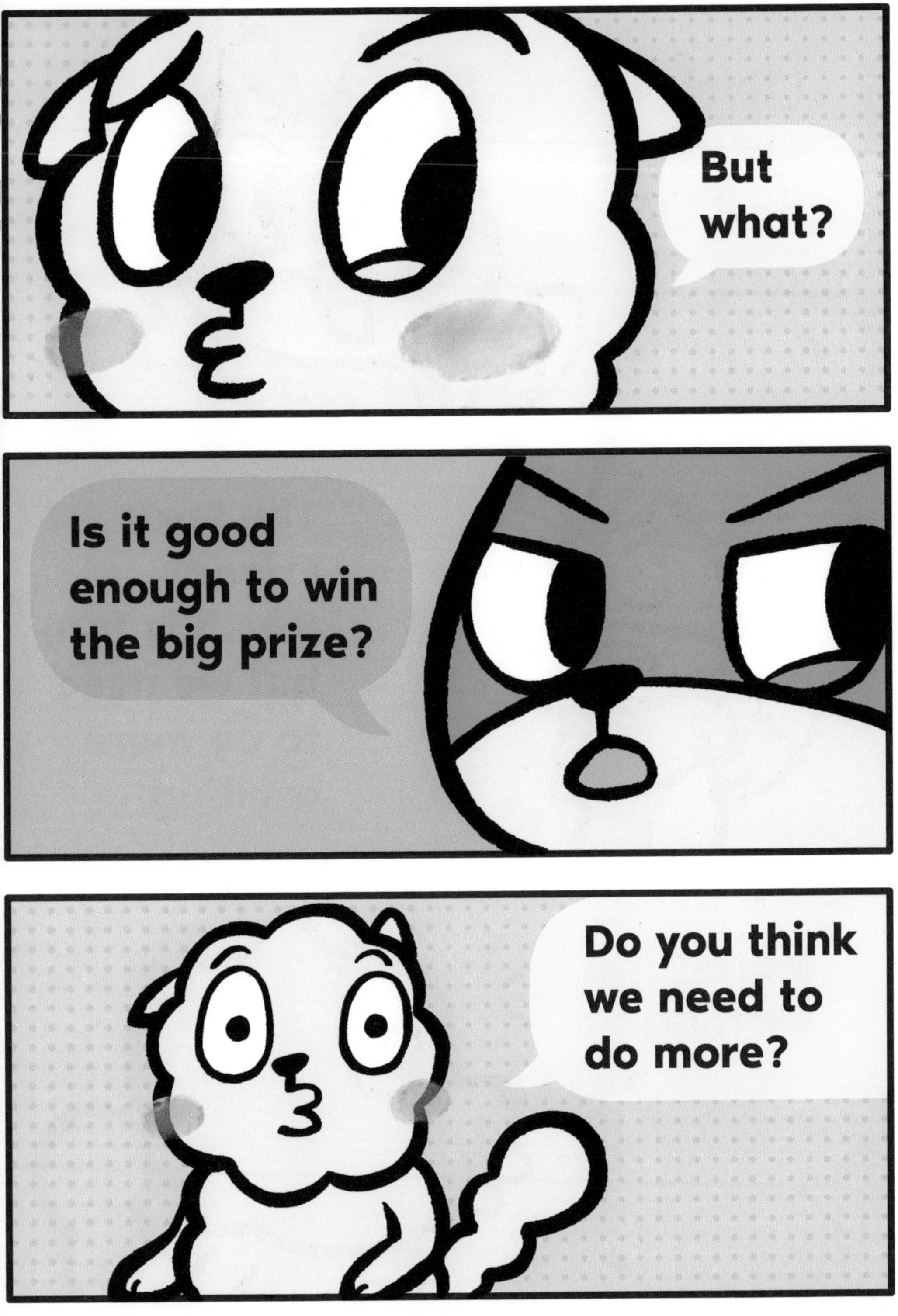
But what?
Is it good enough to win the big prize?
Do you think we need to do more?

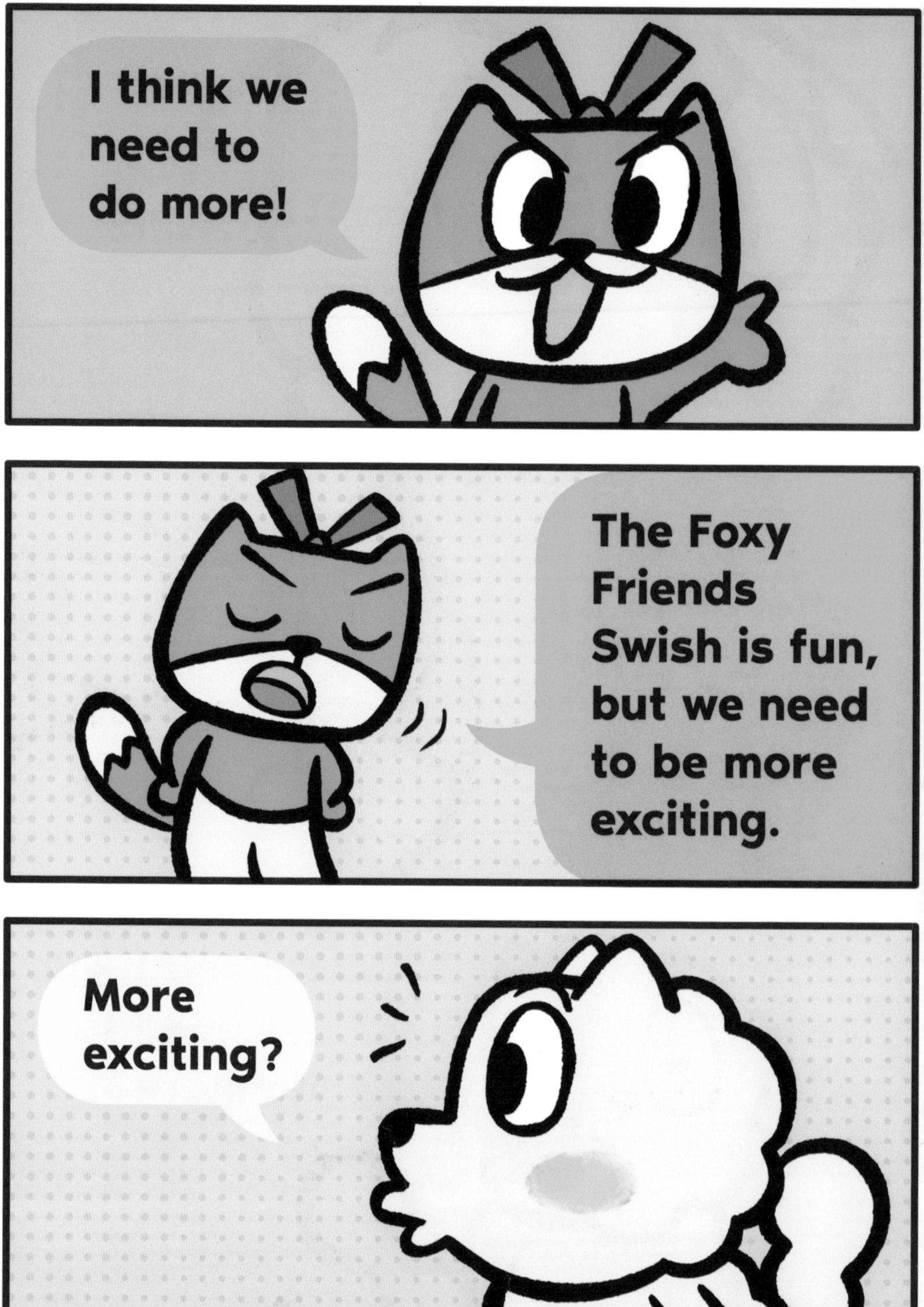
I think we need to do more!
The Foxy Friends Swish is fun, but we need to be more exciting.
More exciting?

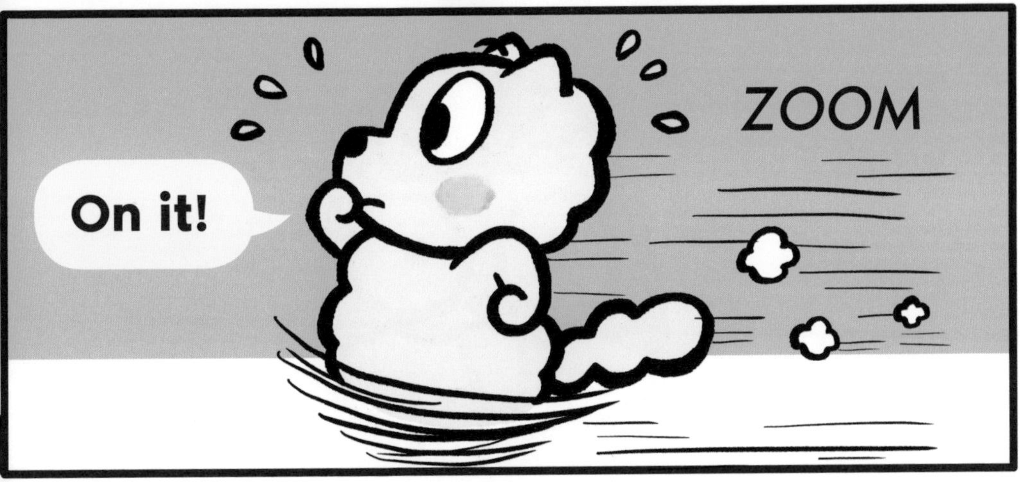
On it!
ZOOM

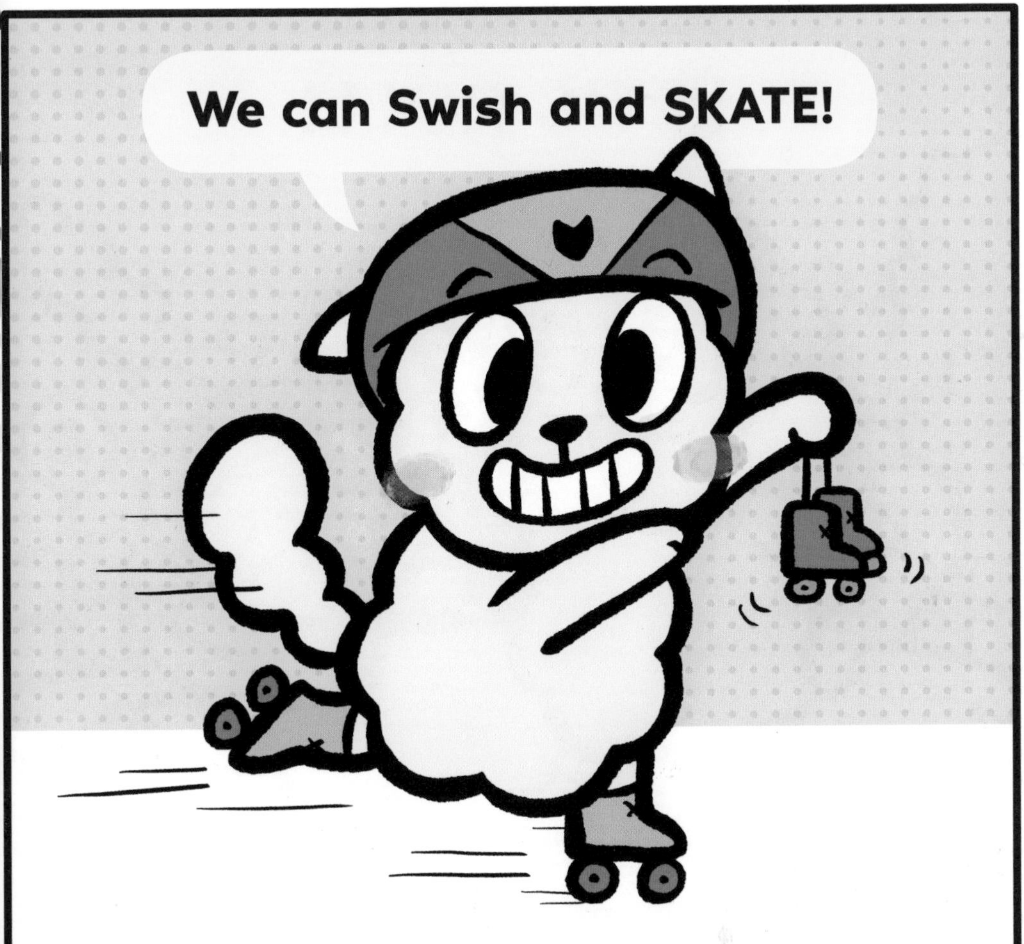
We can Swish and SKATE!

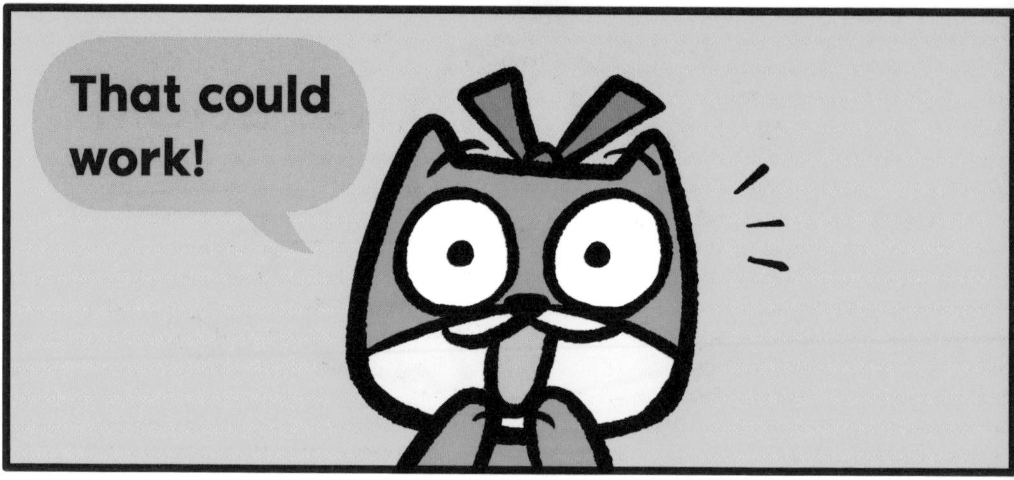
That could work!

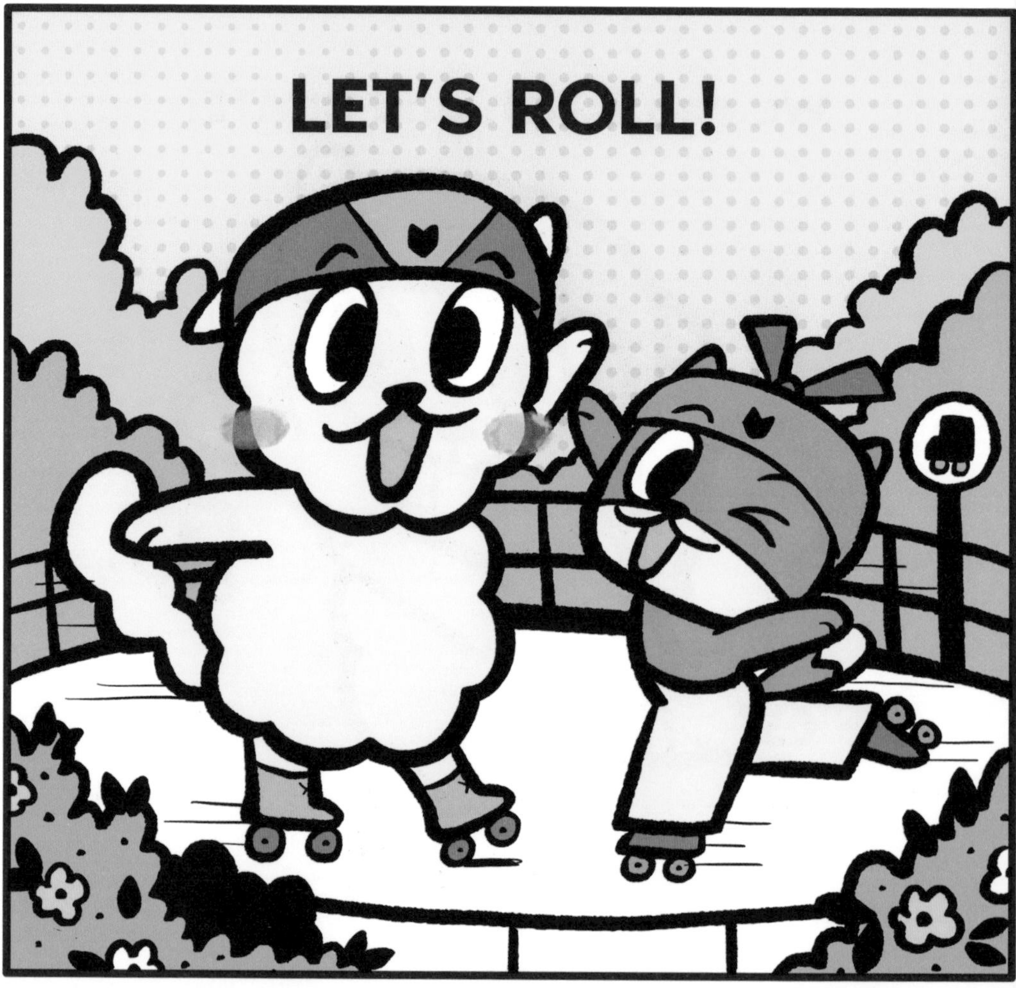
LET'S ROLL!

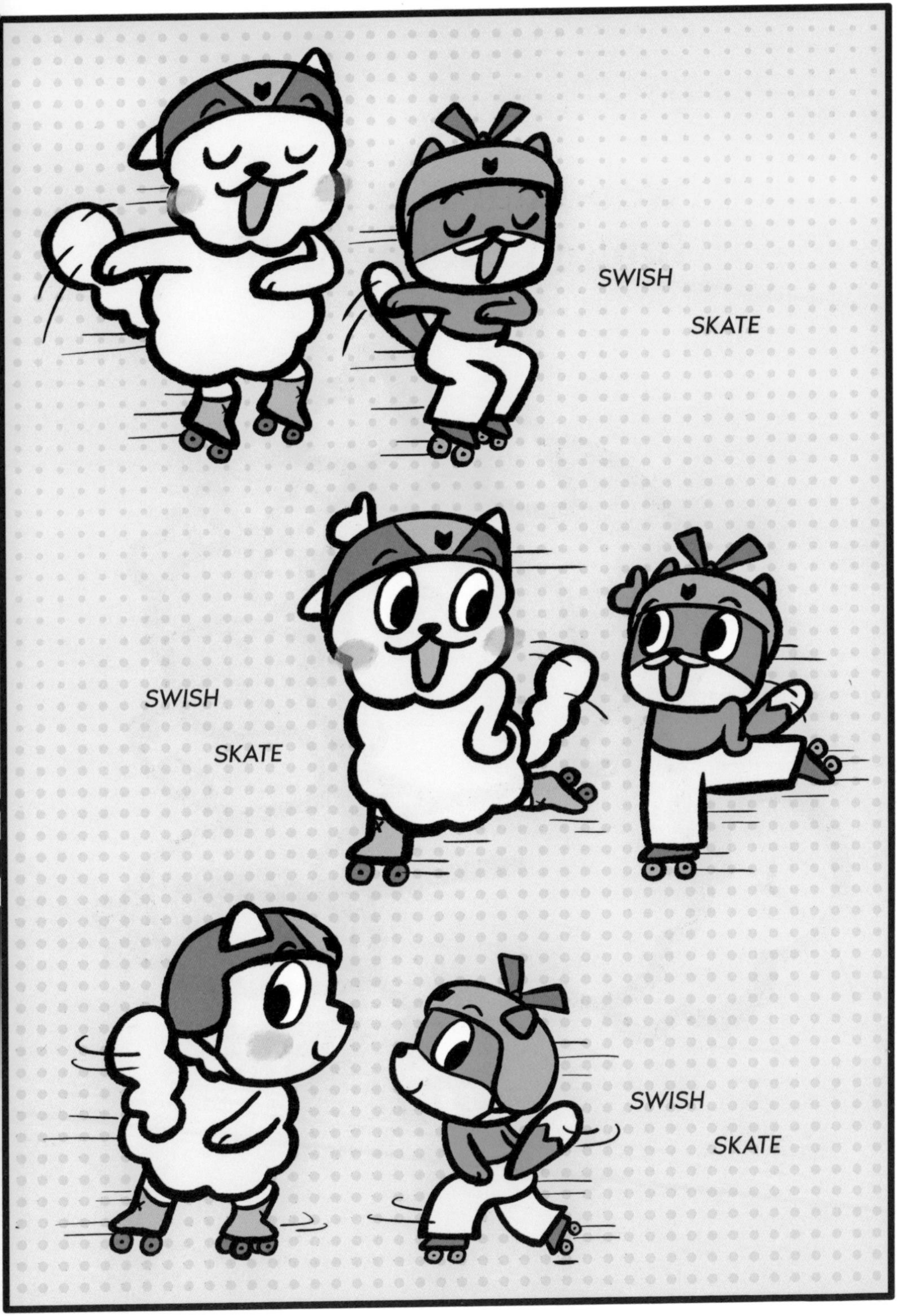
SWISH
SKATE
SWISH
SKATE
SWISH
SKATE

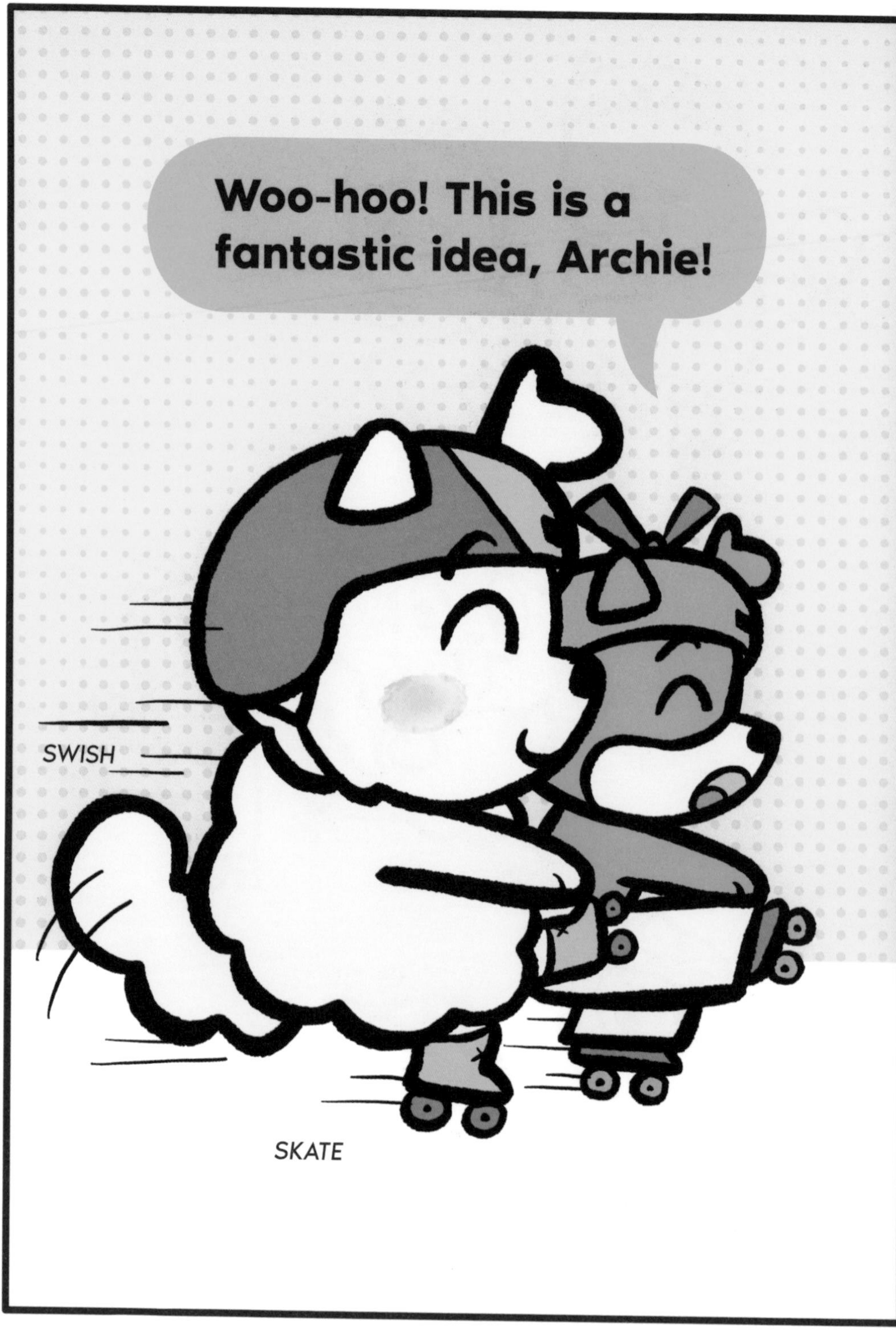
Woo-hoo! This is a fantastic idea, Archie!
SWISH
SKATE

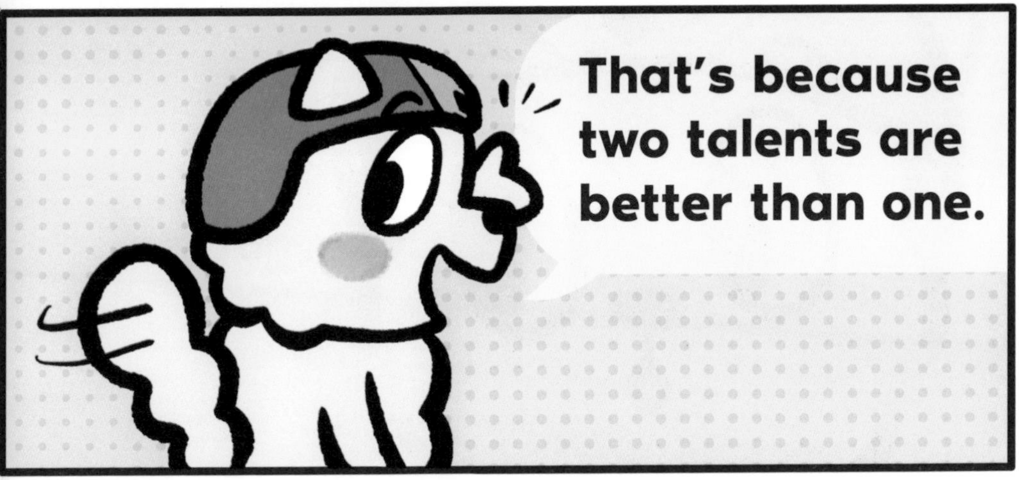
That's because two talents are better than one.

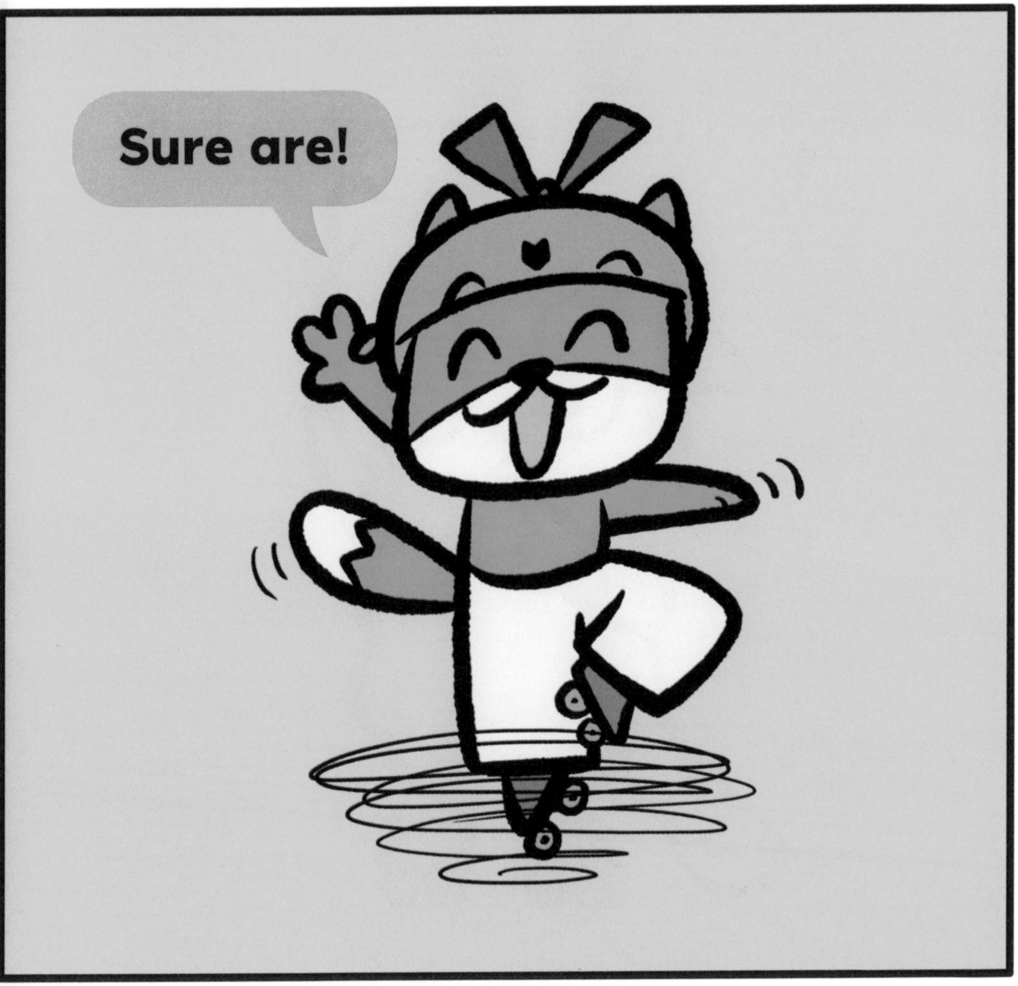
Sure are!

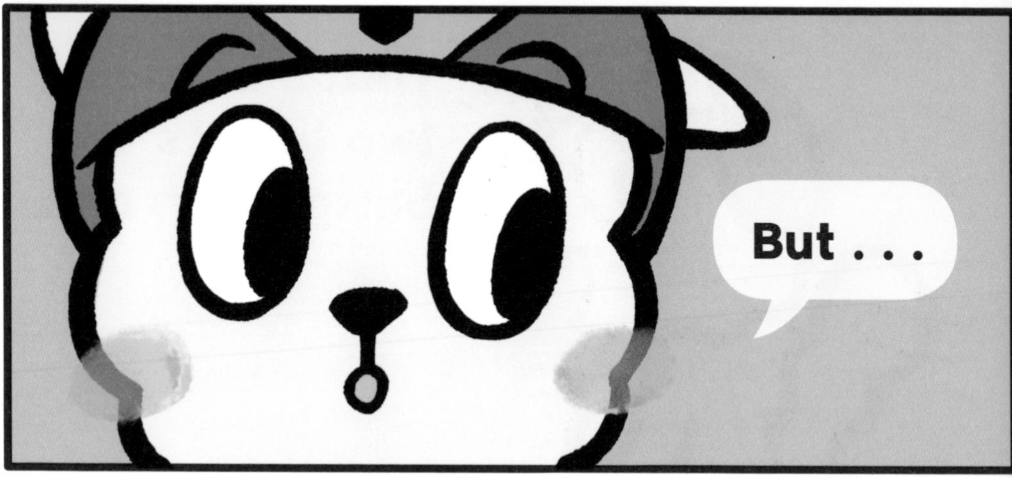
But . . .

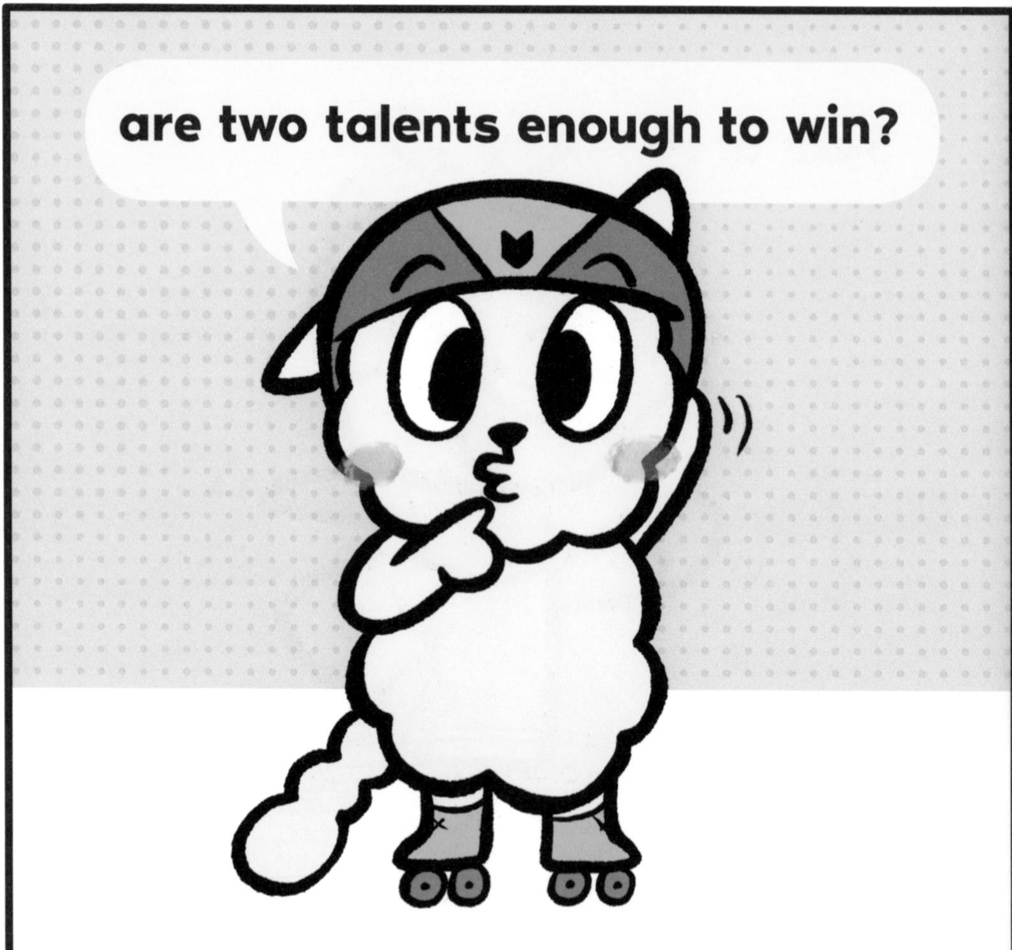
are two talents enough to win?

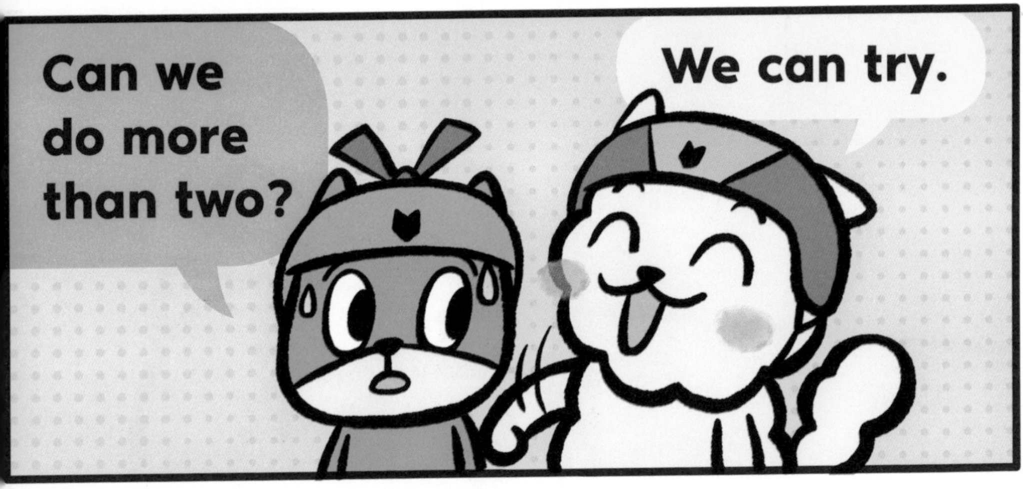
Can we do more than two?
We can try.

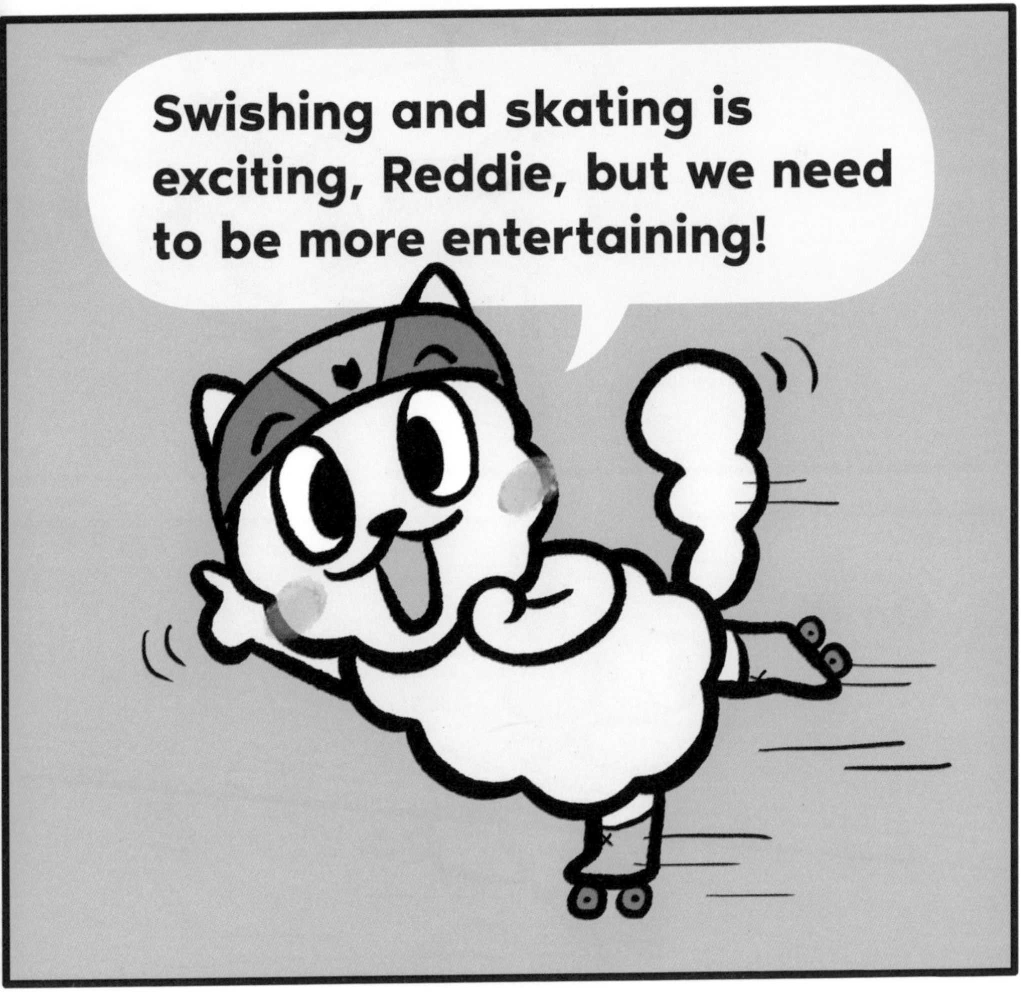
Swishing and skating is exciting, Reddie, but we need to be more entertaining!

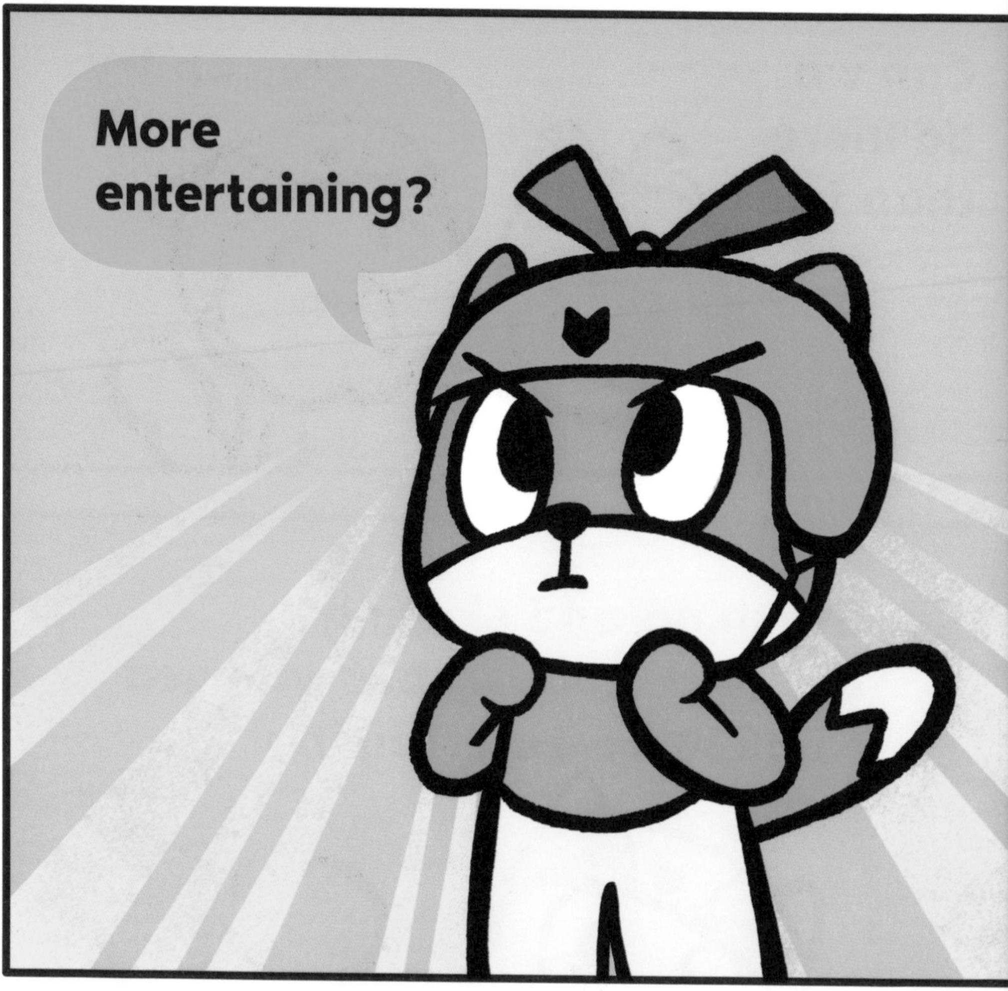
More entertaining?

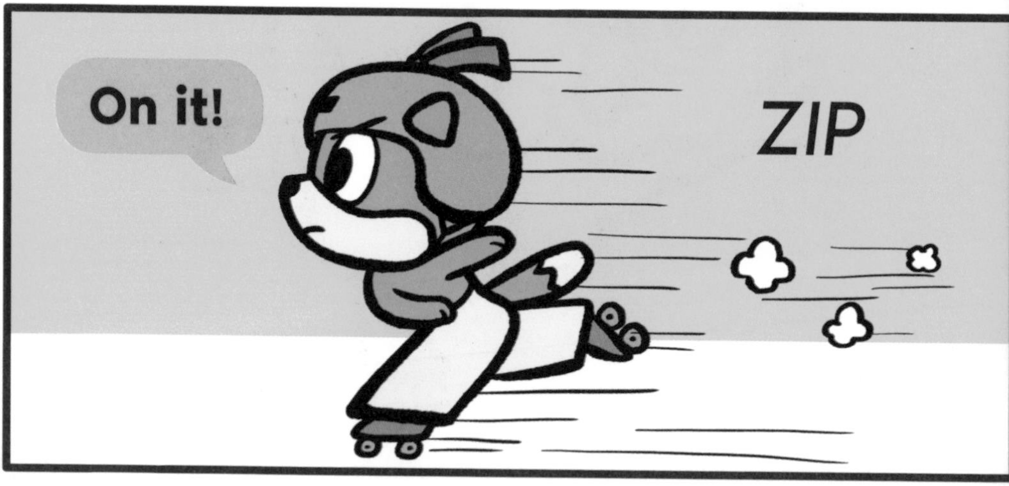
On it!
ZIP

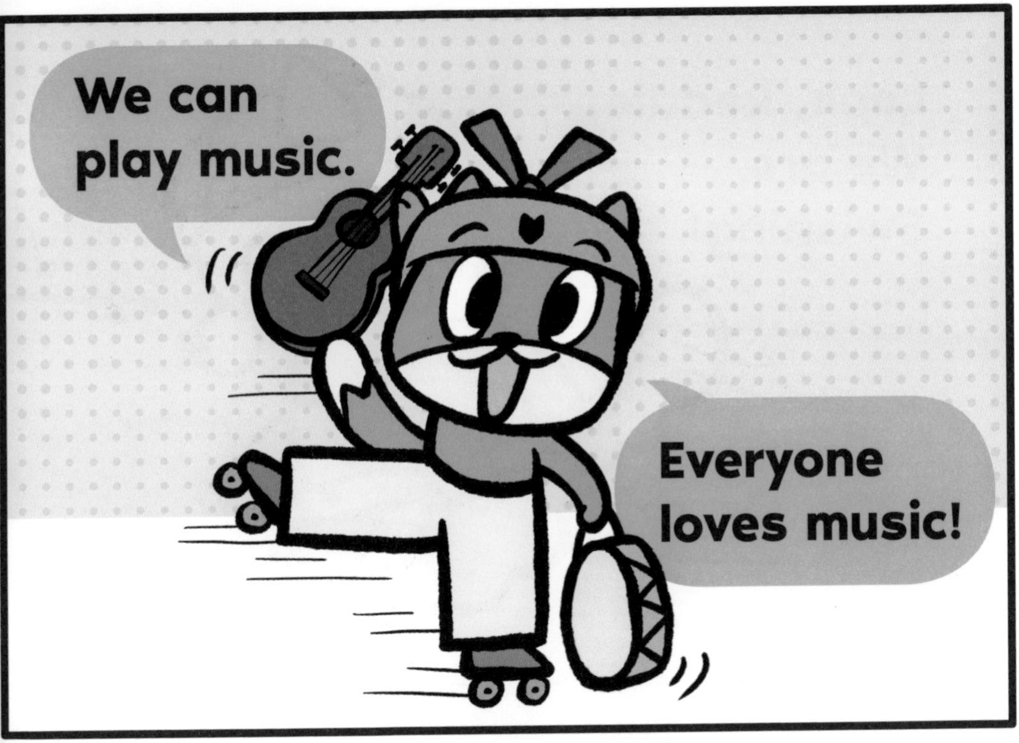
We can play music.
Everyone loves music!

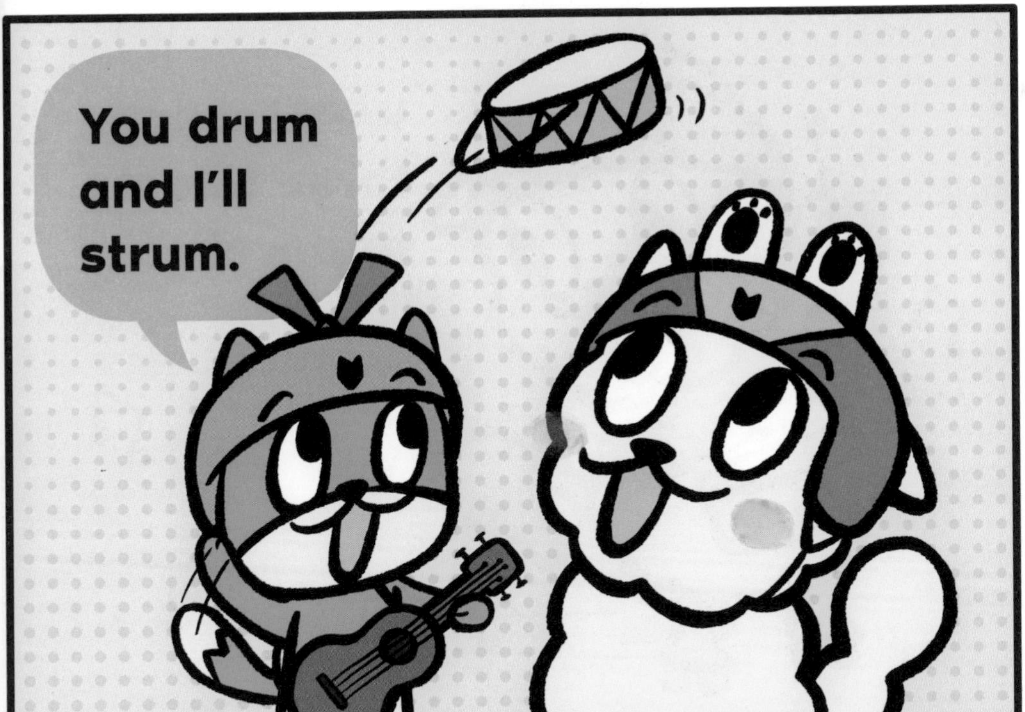
You drum and I'll strum.

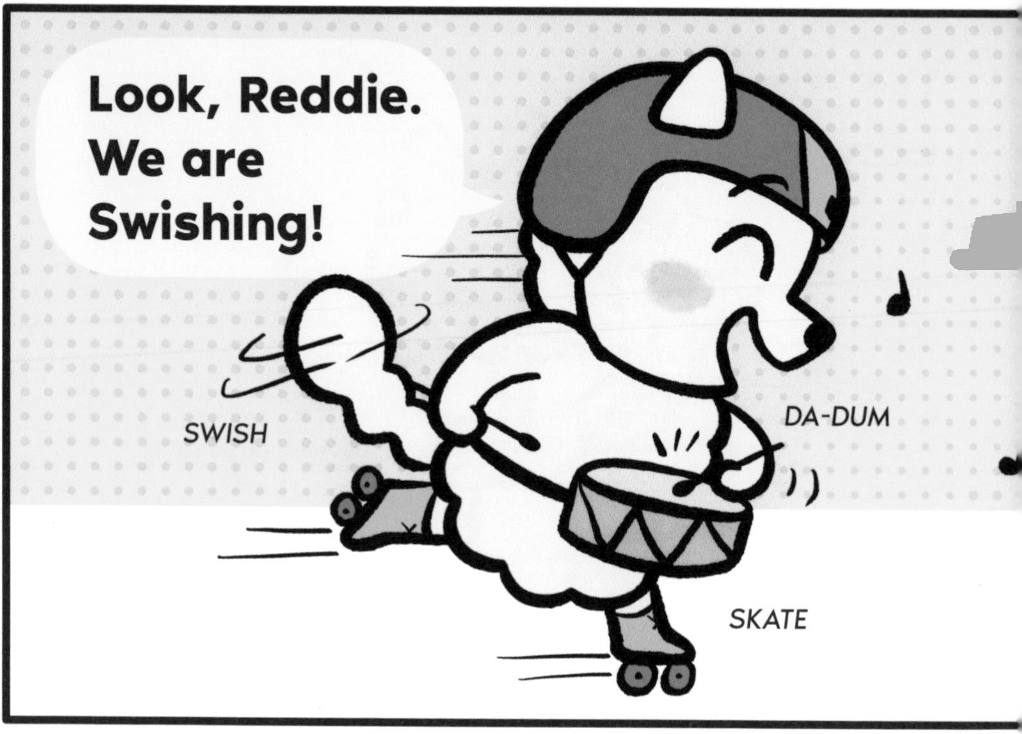
Look, Reddie.
We are
Swishing!
SWISH
DA-DUM
SKATE

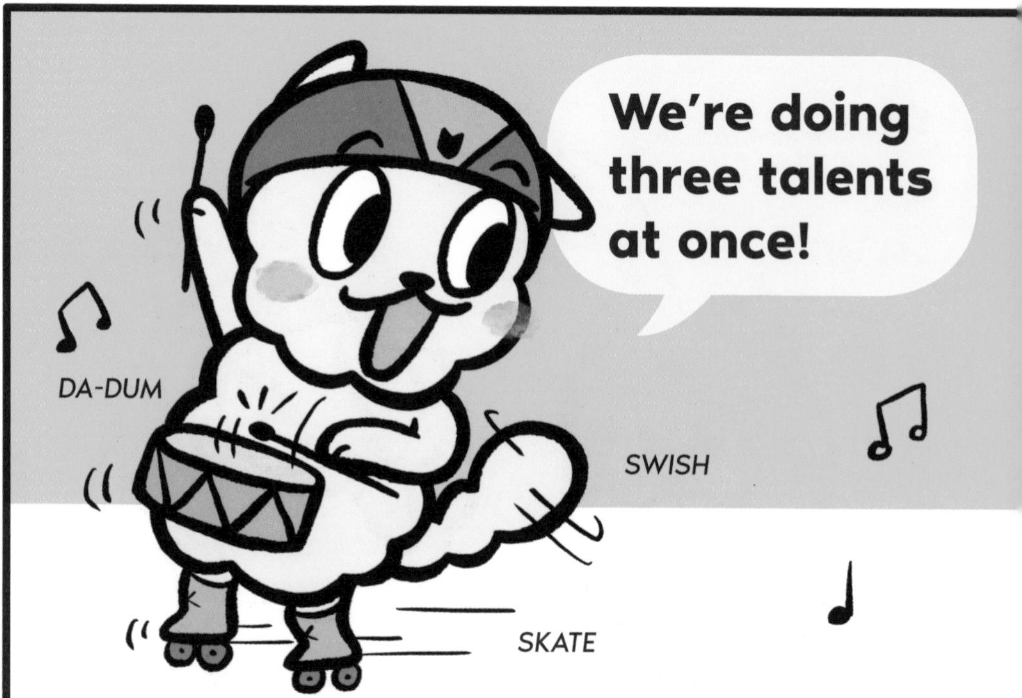
We're doing
three talents
at once!
DA-DUM
SWISH
SKATE

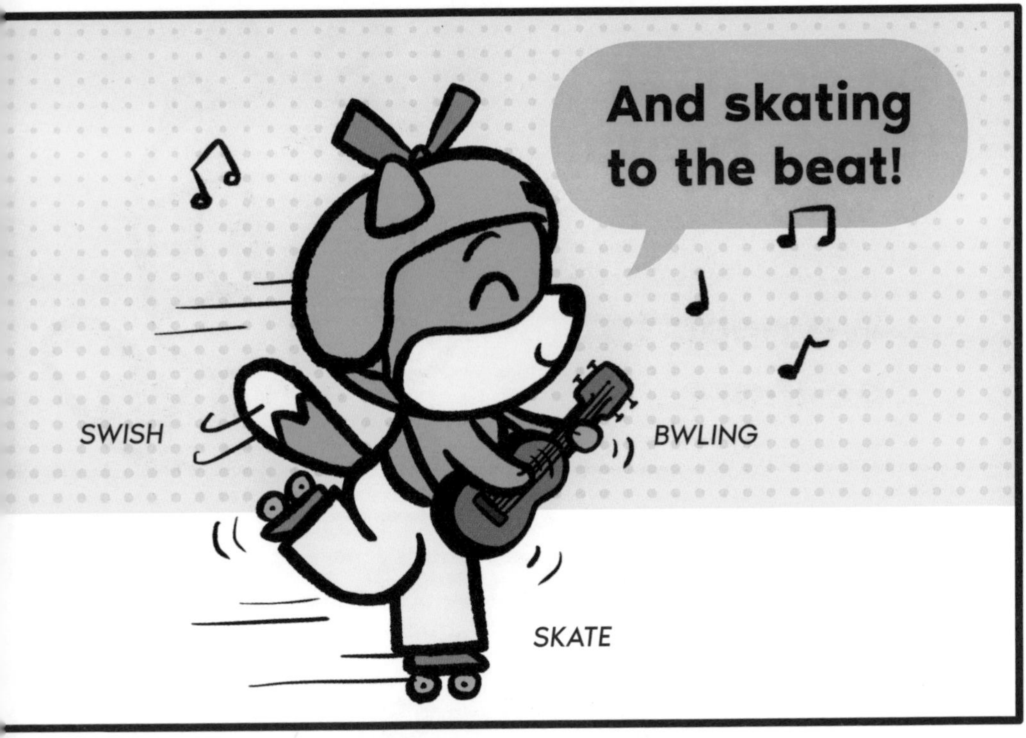
And skating to the beat!
SWISH
BWLING
SKATE

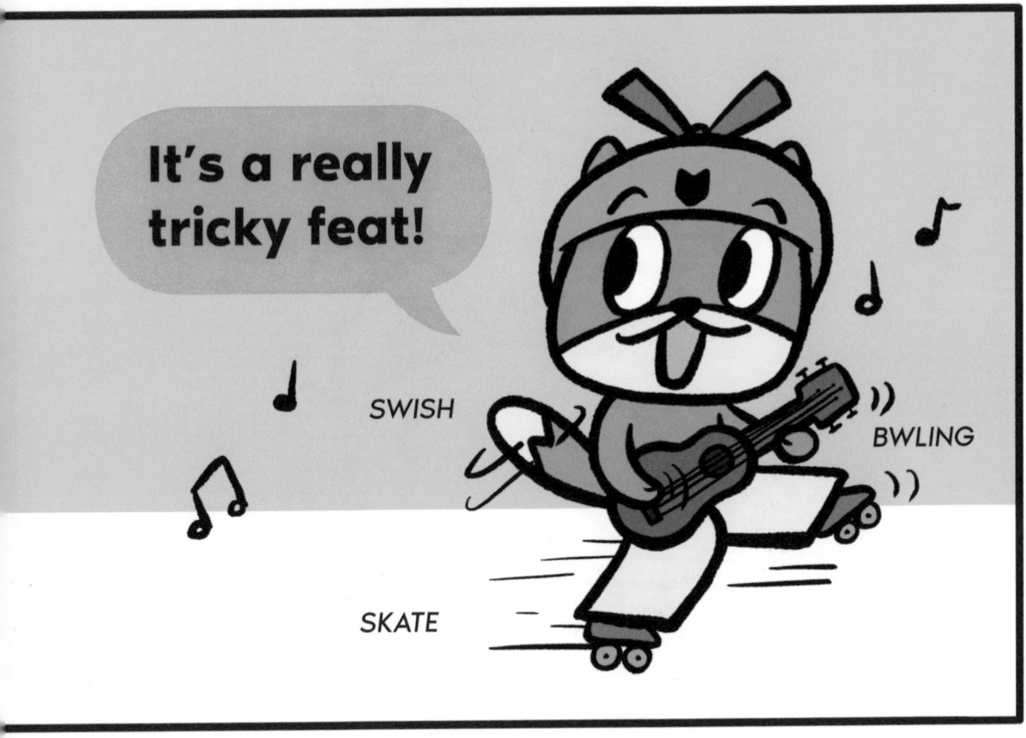
It's a really tricky feat!
SWISH
BWLING
SKATE

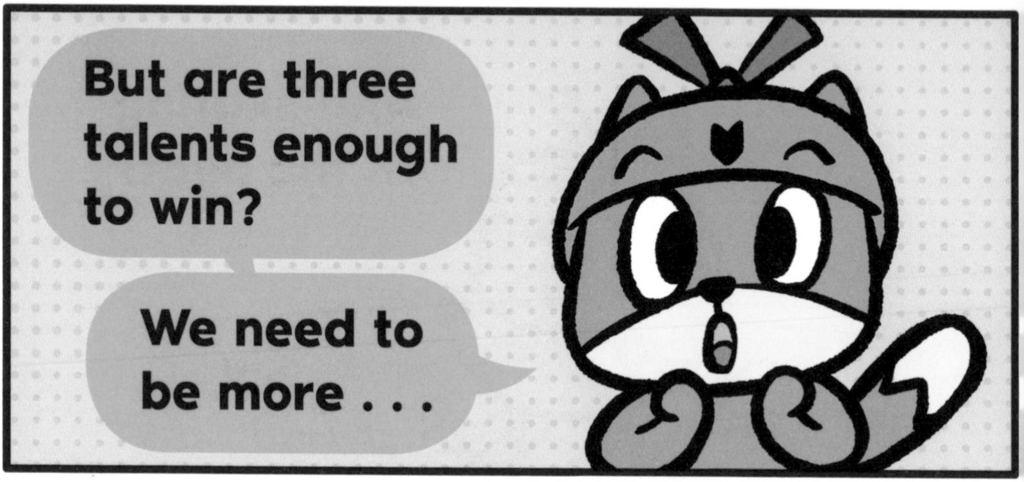
But are three talents enough to win?
We need to be more . . .

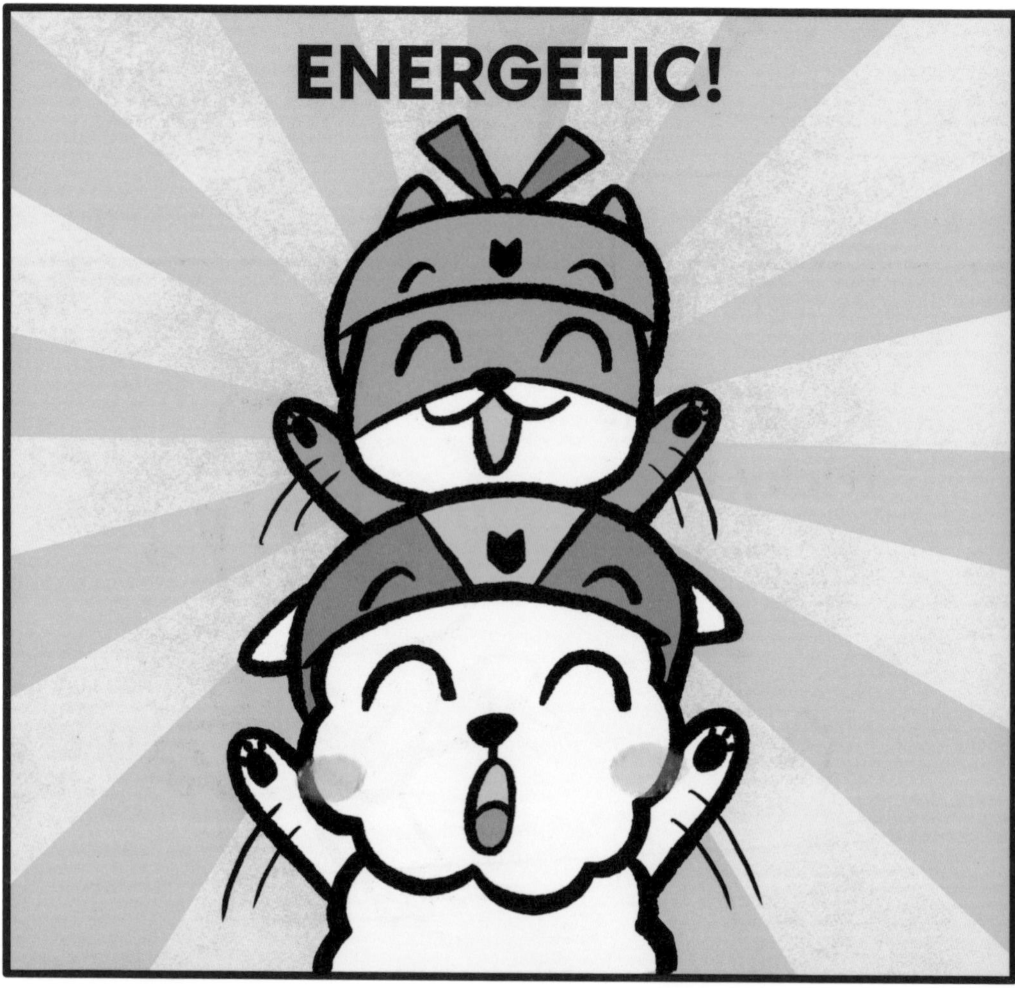
ENERGETIC!

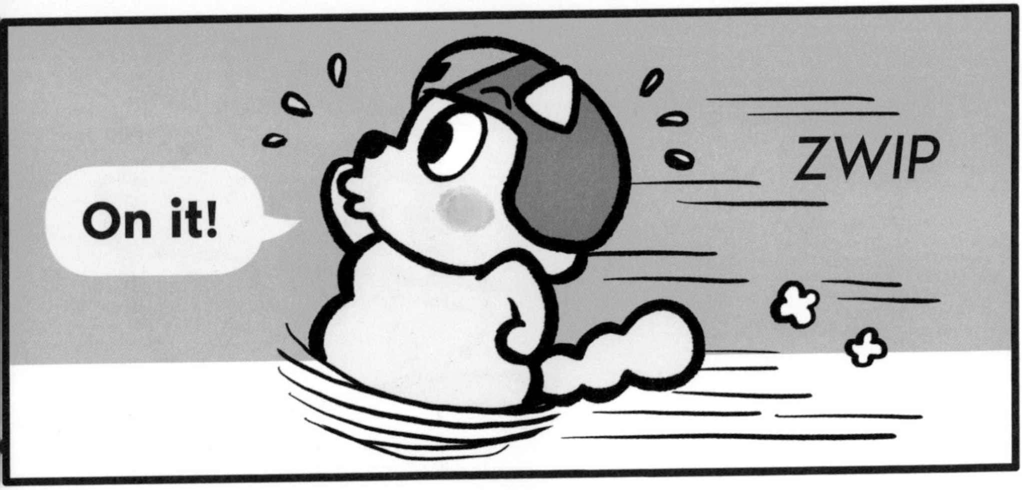
On it!
ZWIP

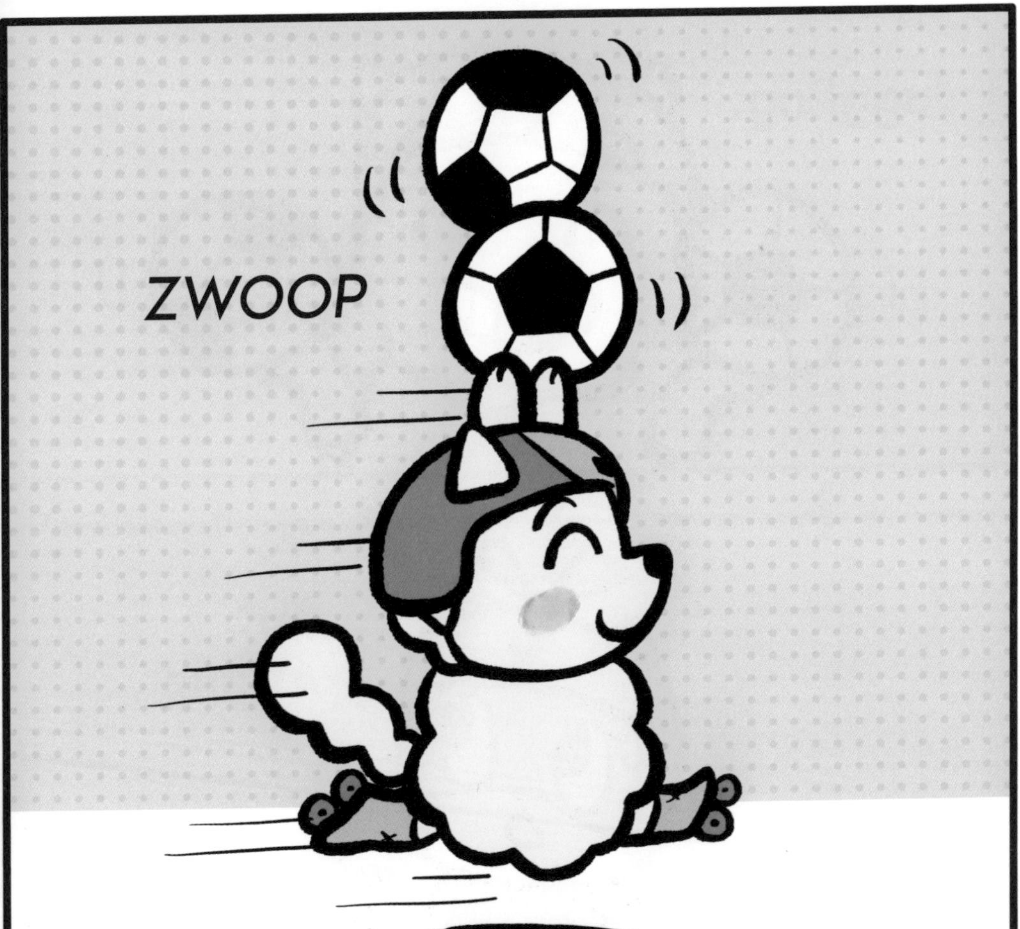
ZWOOP

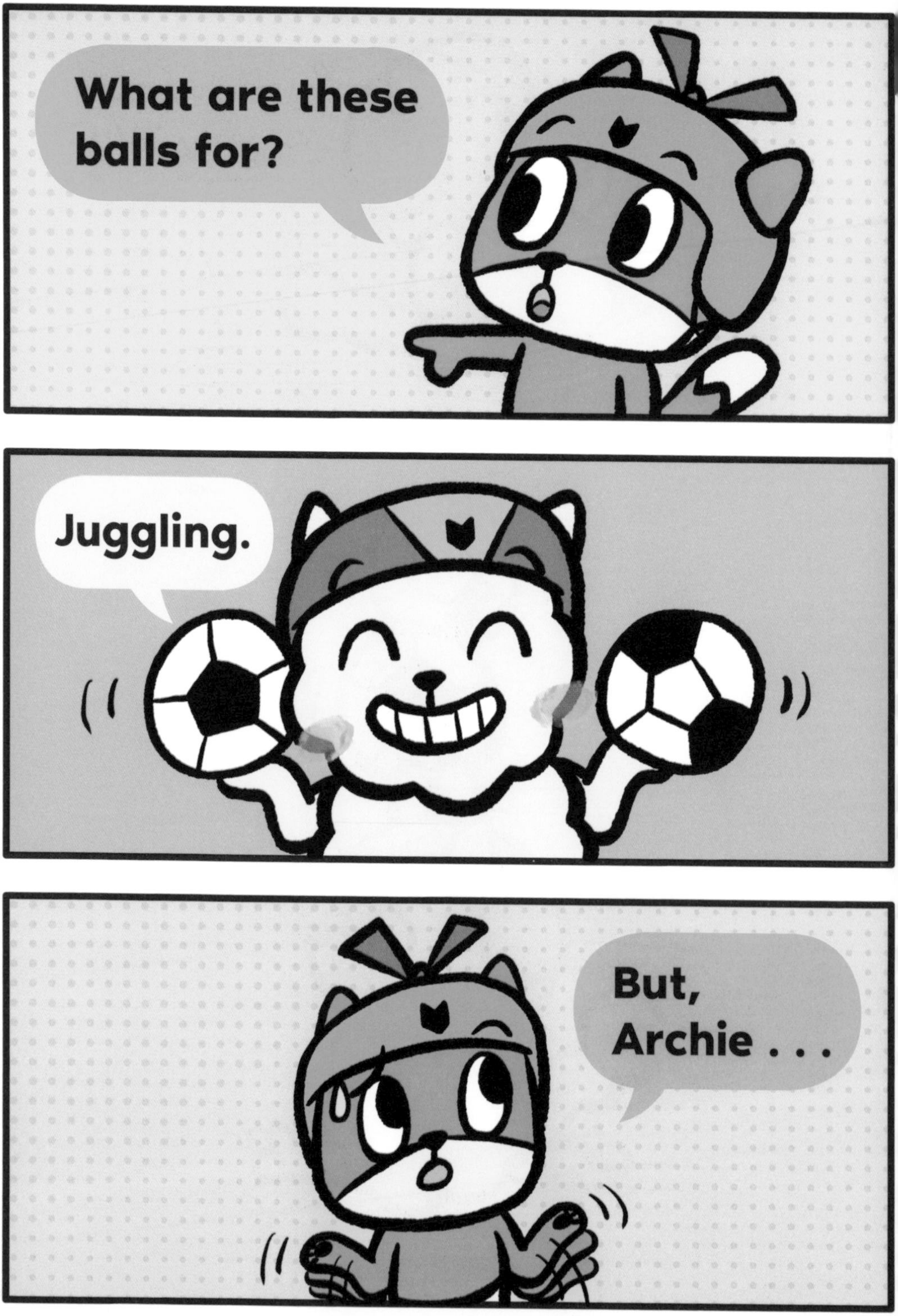
What are these balls for?
Juggling.
But, Archie . . .

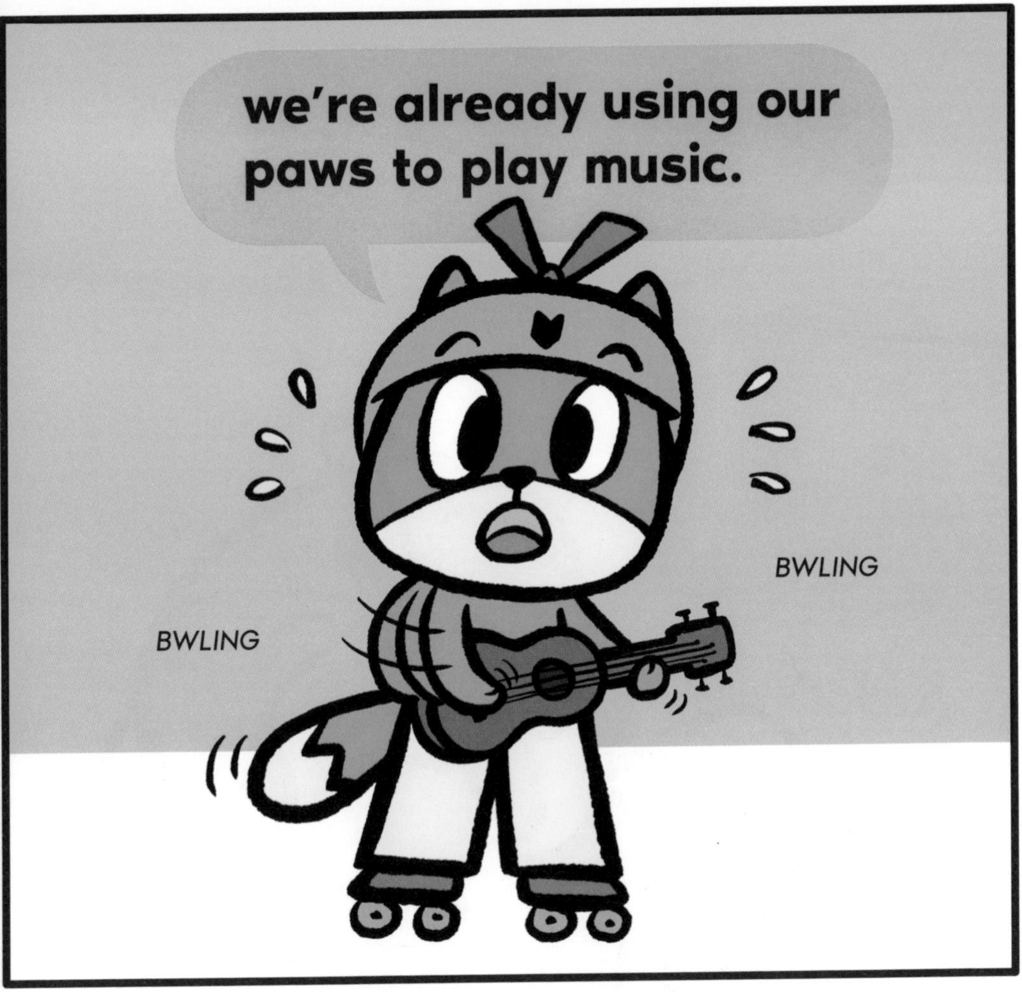
we're already using our paws to play music.
BWLING
BWLING

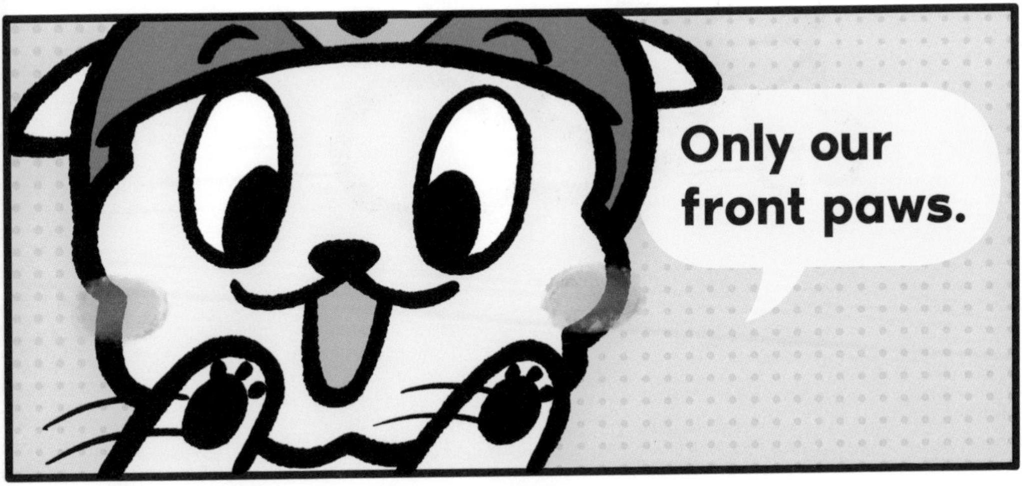
Only our front paws.

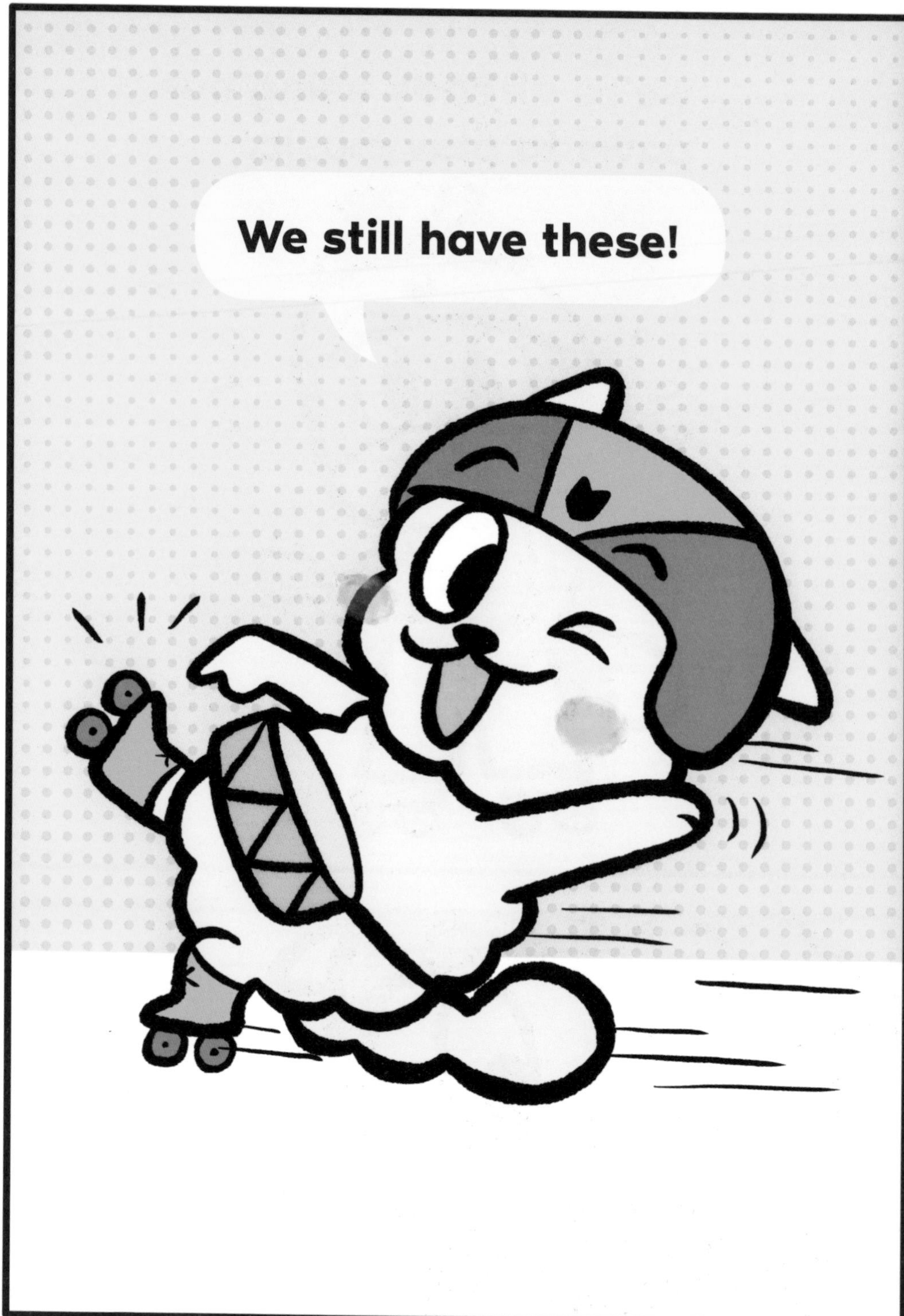
We still have these!

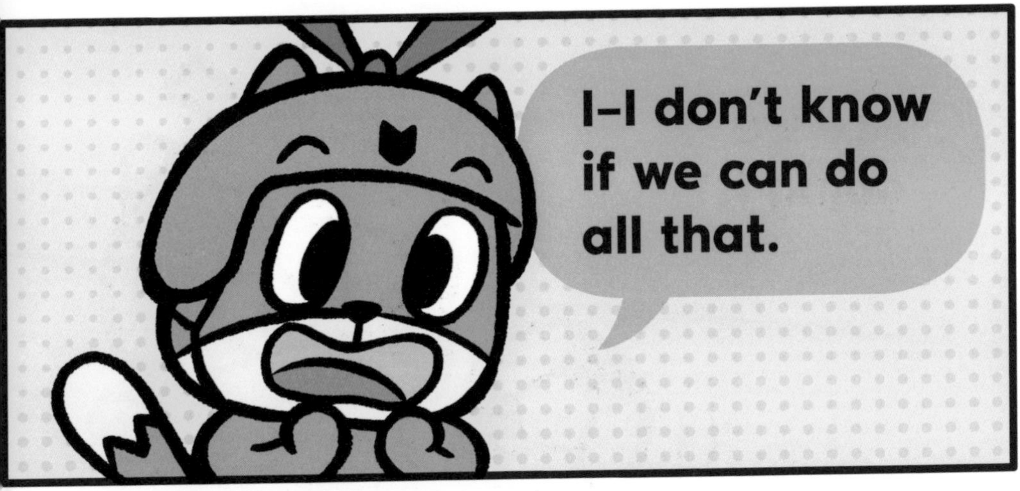
I–I don't know if we can do all that.

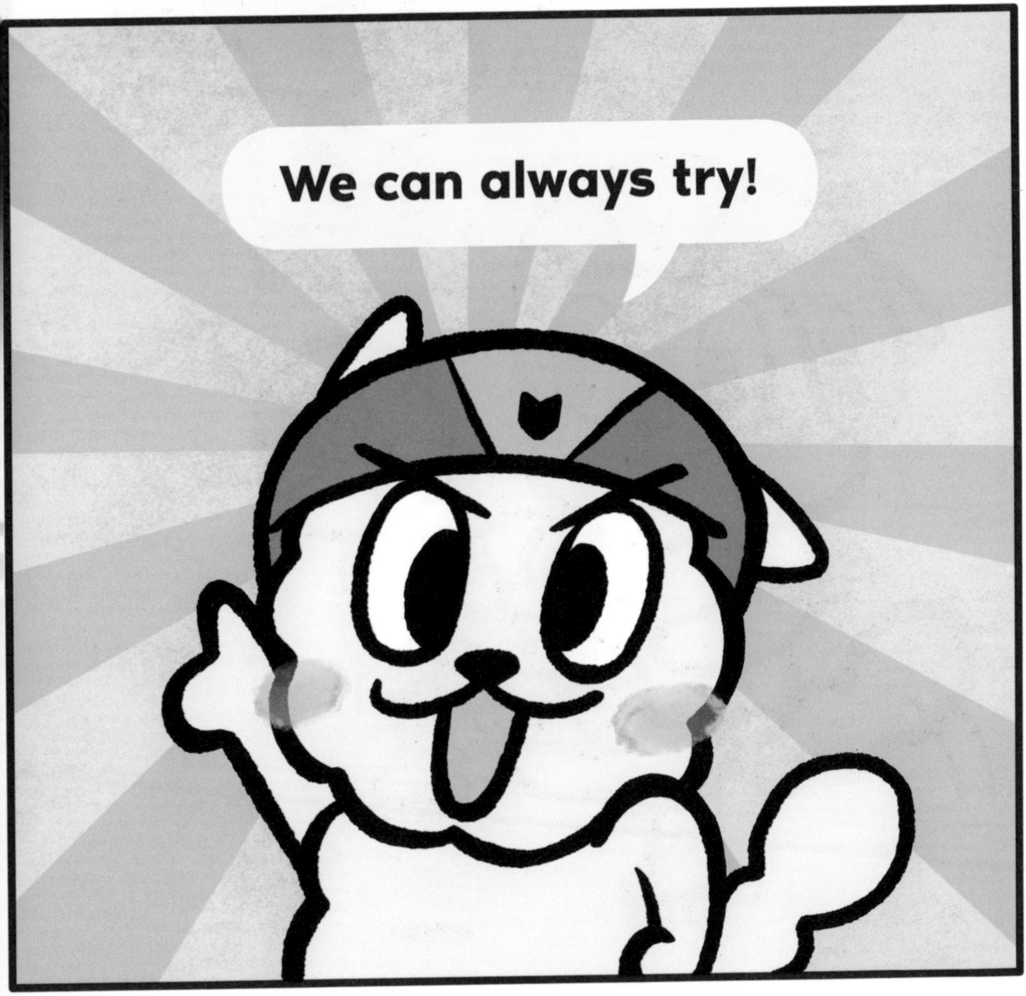
We can always try!

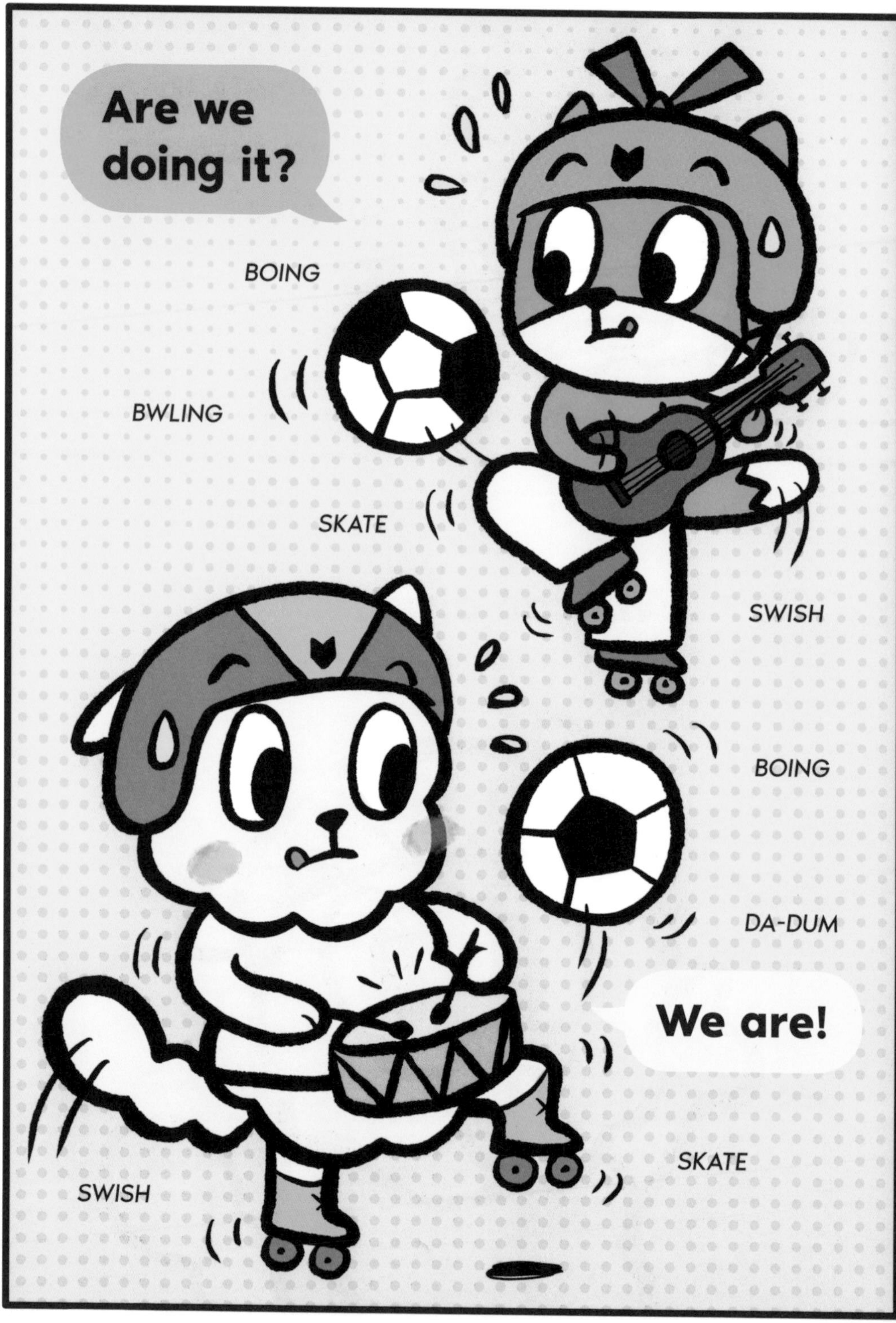
Are we doing it?
BOING
BWLING
SKATE
SWISH
BOING
DA-DUM
We are!
SKATE
SWISH

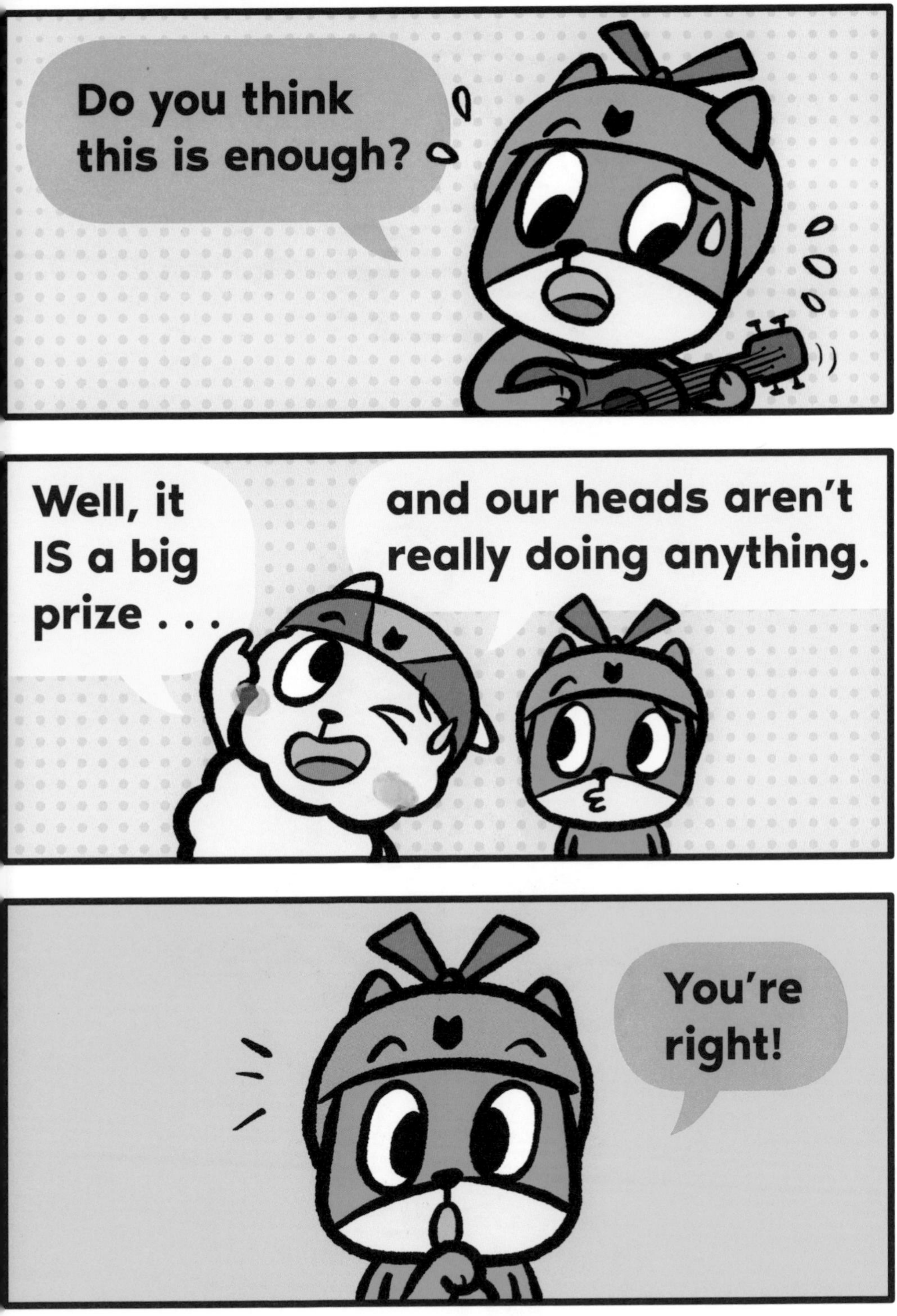

Do you think this is enough?
Well, it IS a big prize . . .
and our heads aren't really doing anything.
You're right!

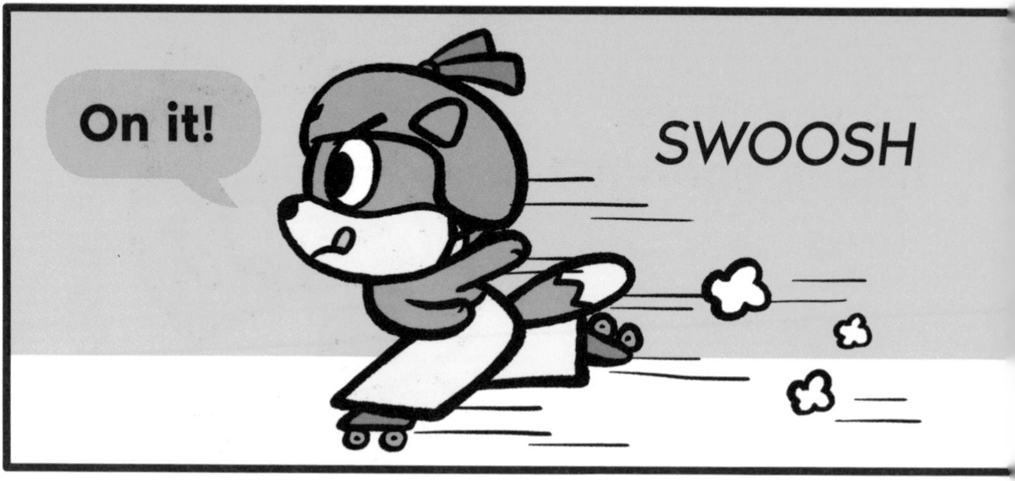
On it!
SWOOSH

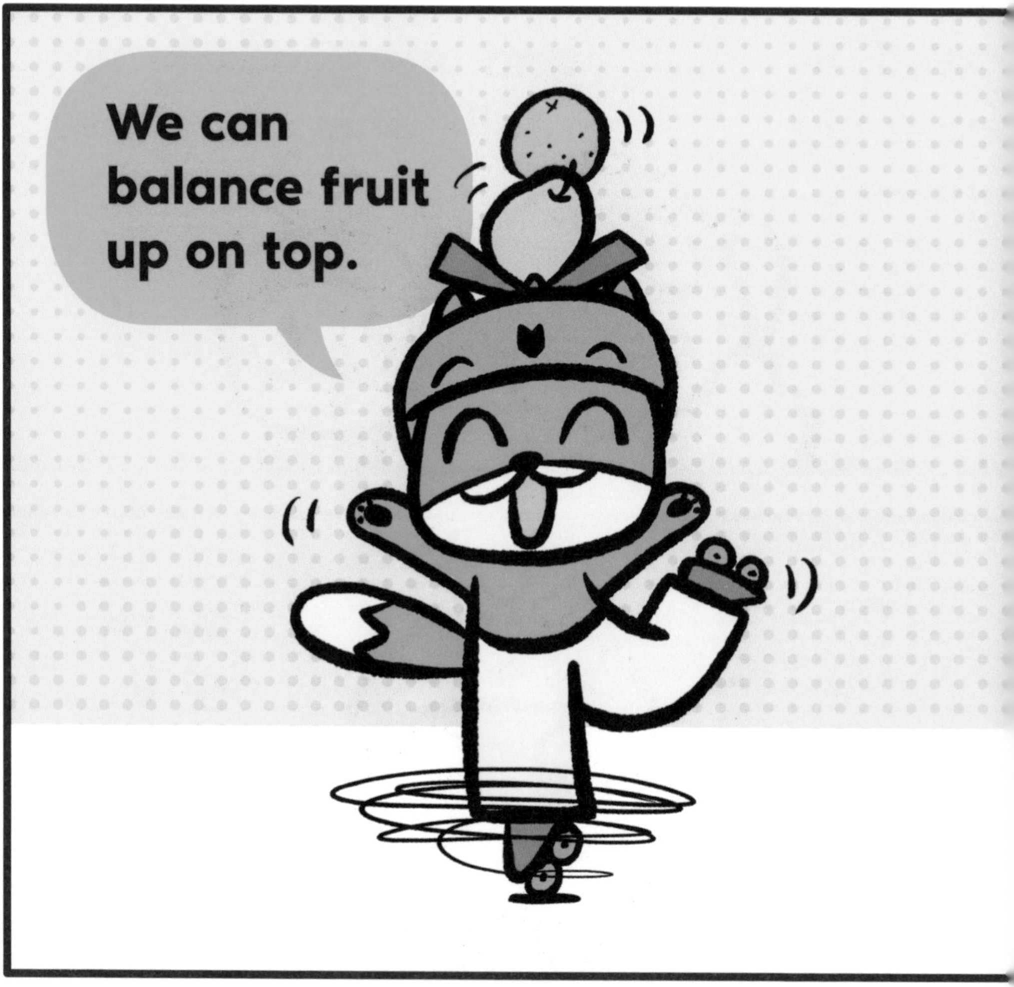
We can balance fruit up on top.

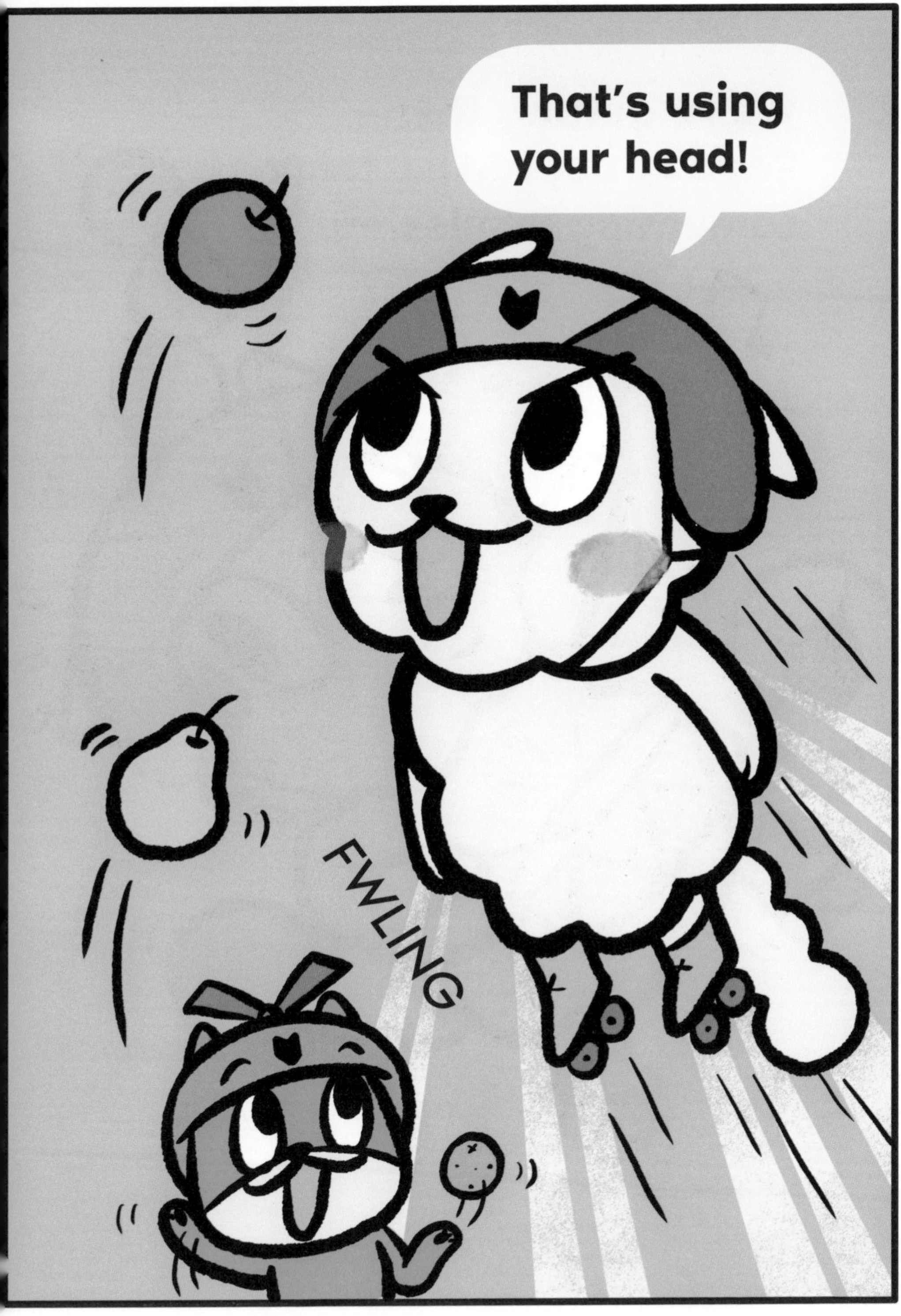
That's using your head!
FWLING

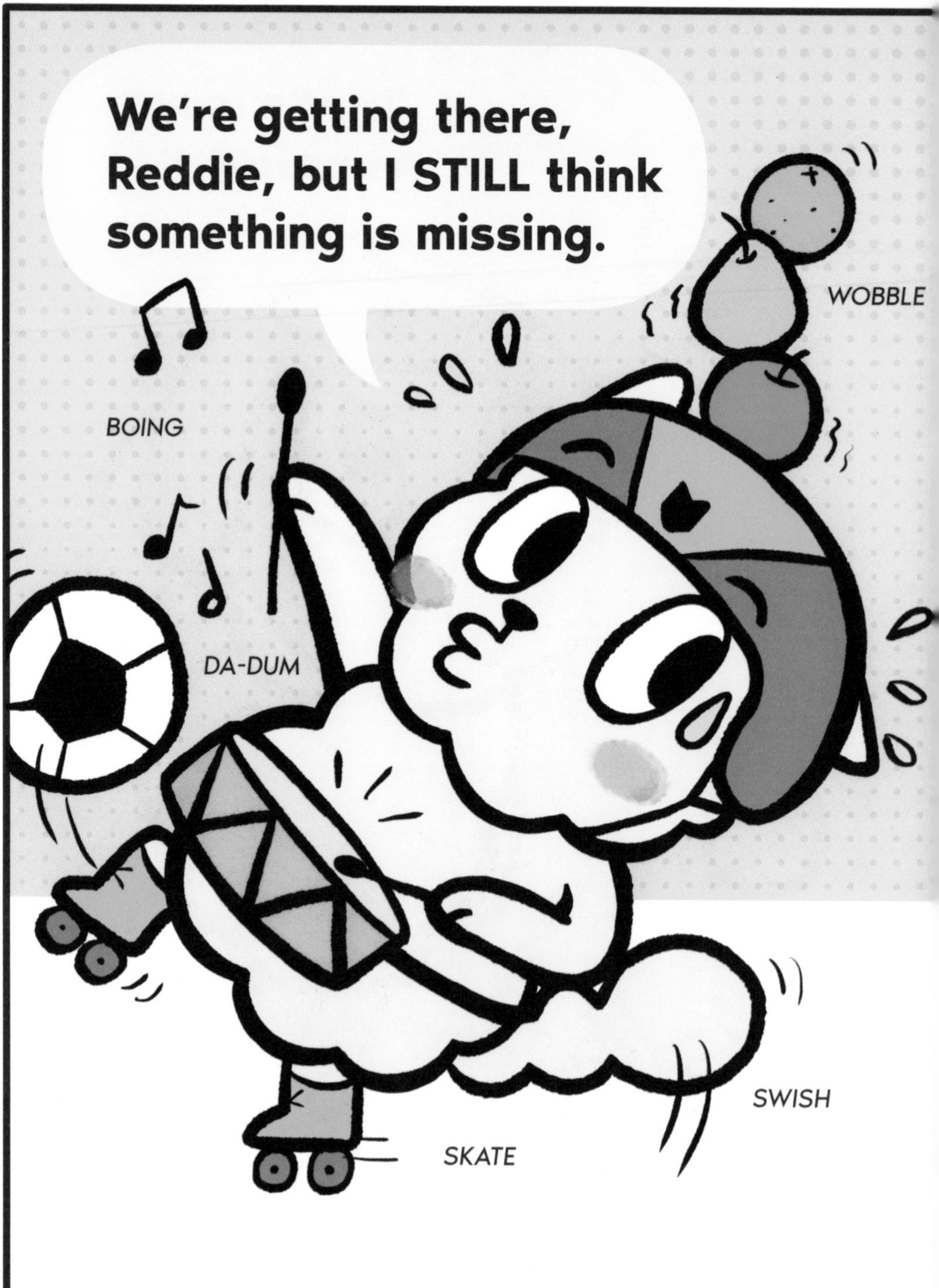
We're getting there, Reddie, but I STILL think something is missing.
WOBBLE
BOING
DA-DUM
SWISH
SKATE

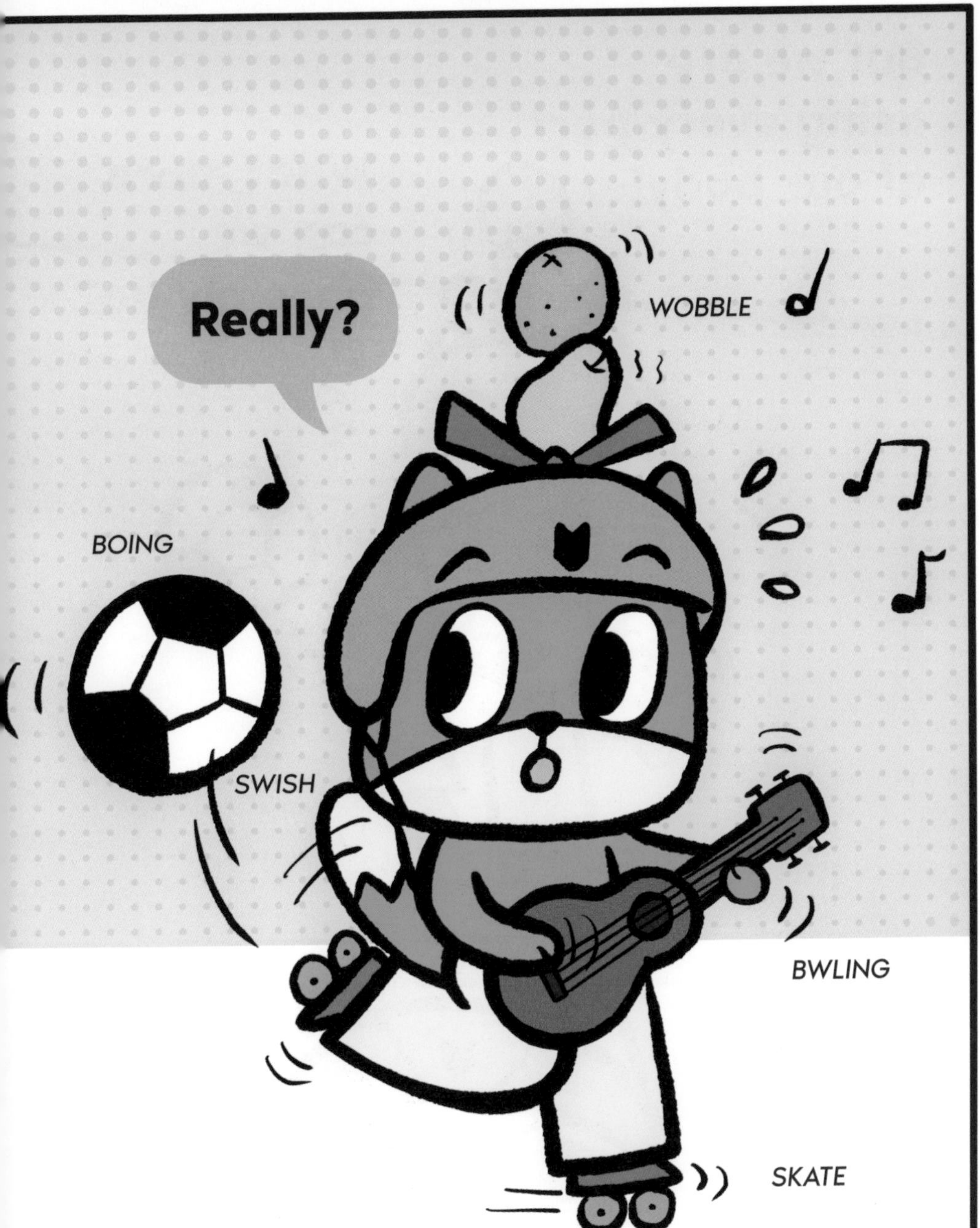
Really?
WOBBLE
BOING
SWISH
BWLING
SKATE

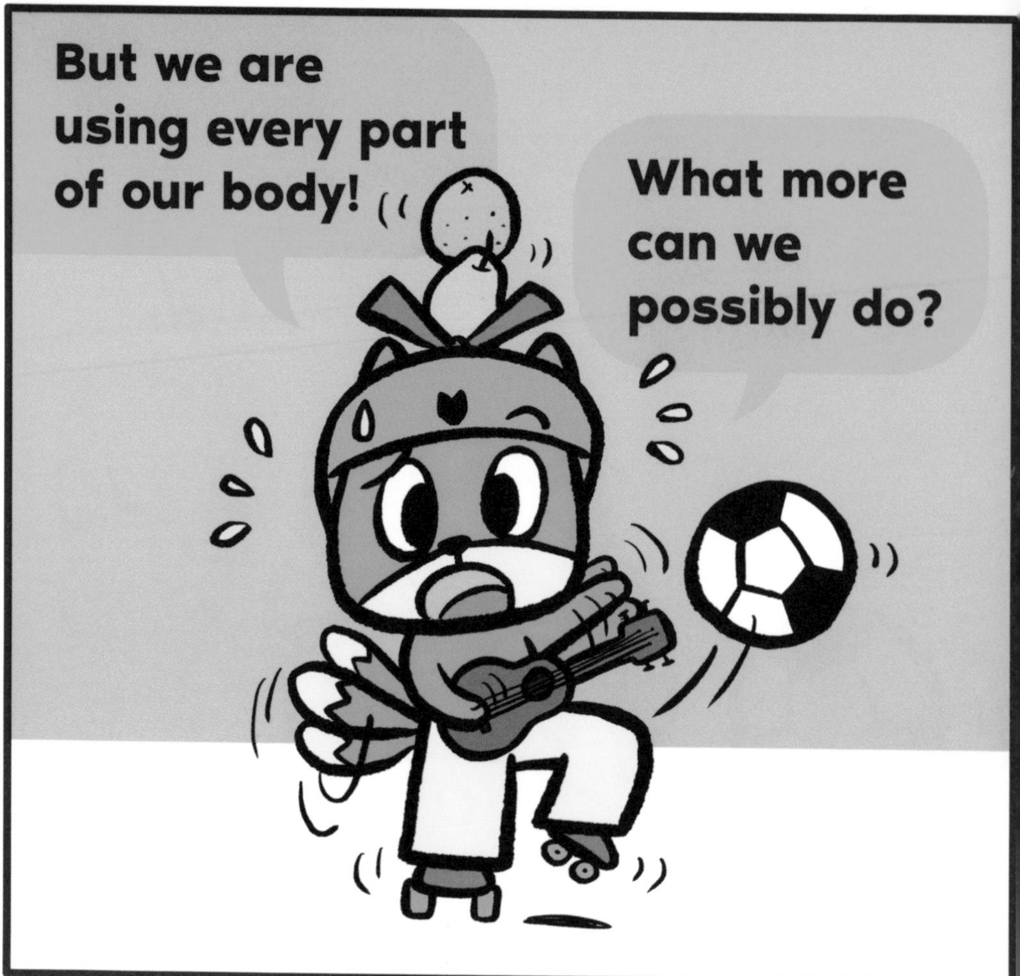
But we are using every part of our body!
What more can we possibly do?

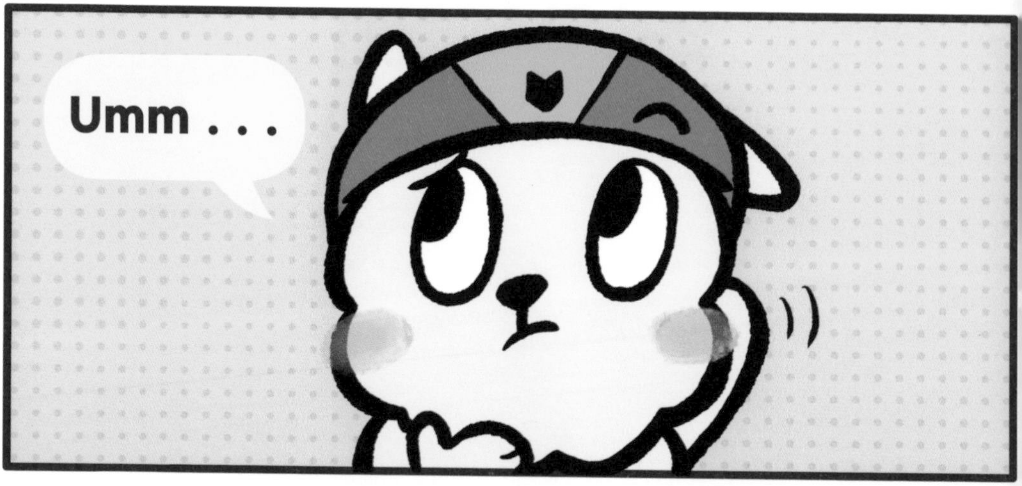
Umm . . .

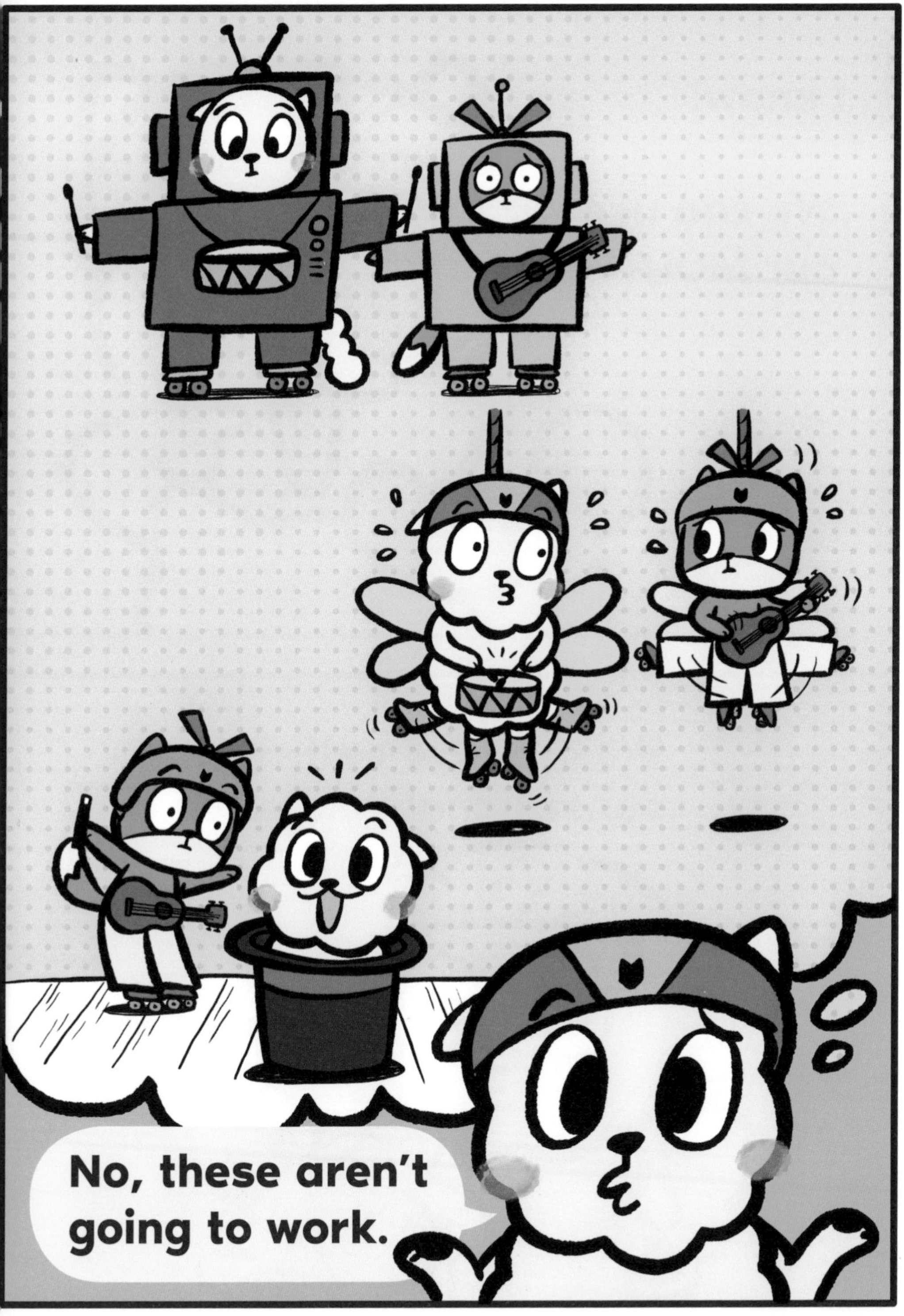
No, these aren't going to work.

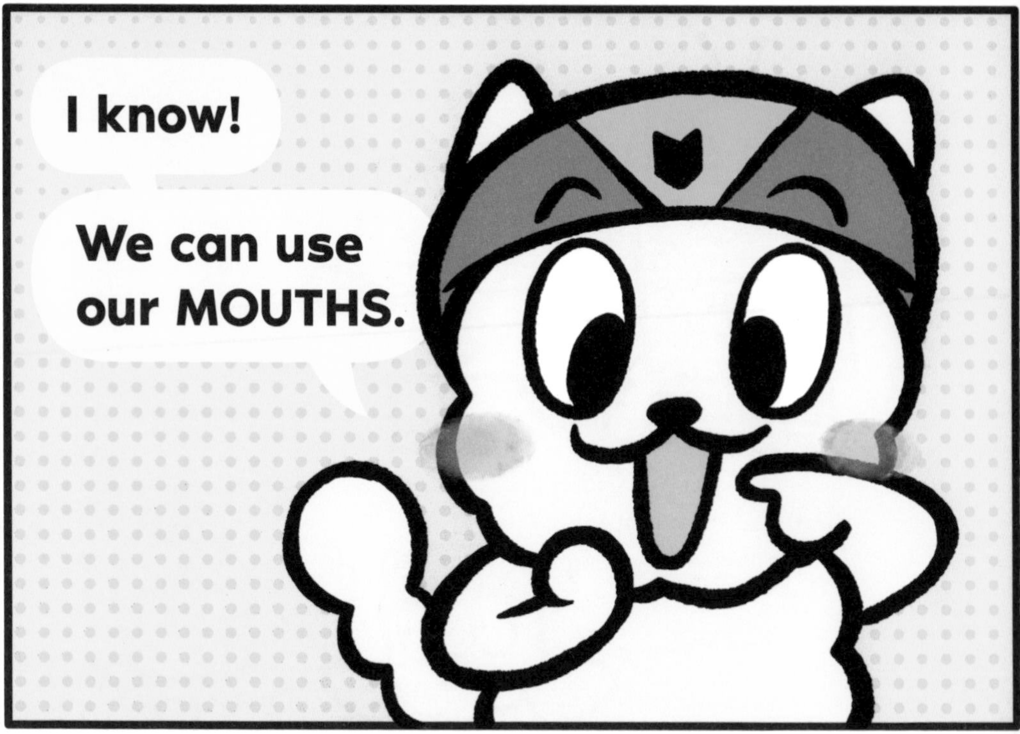
I know!
We can use our MOUTHS.

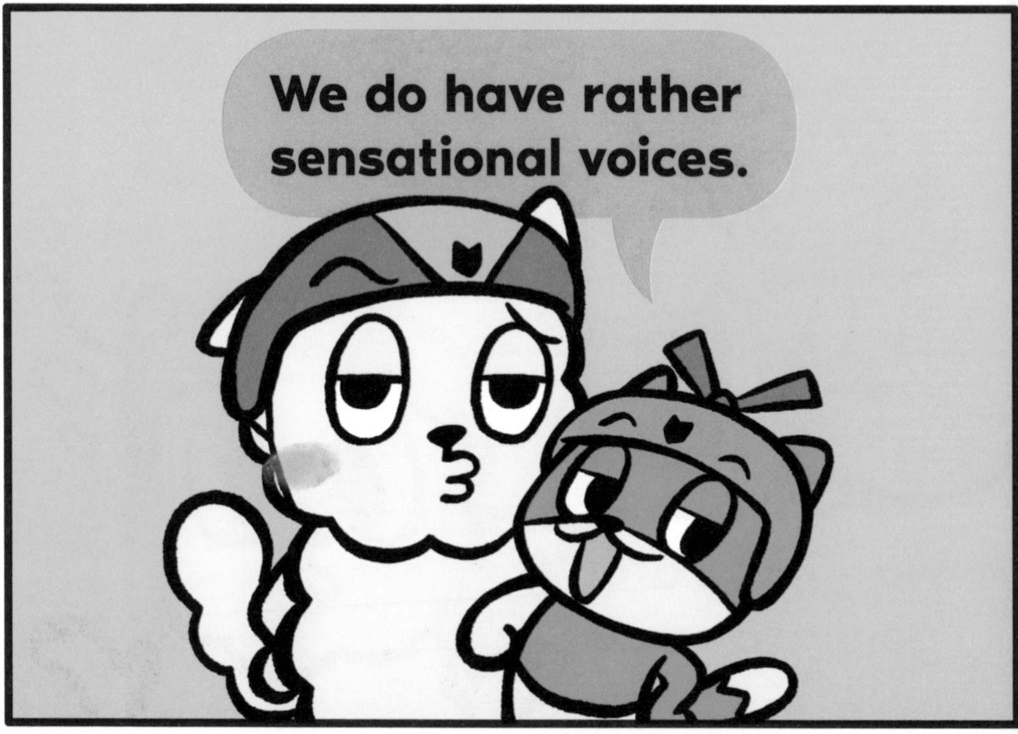
We do have rather sensational voices.

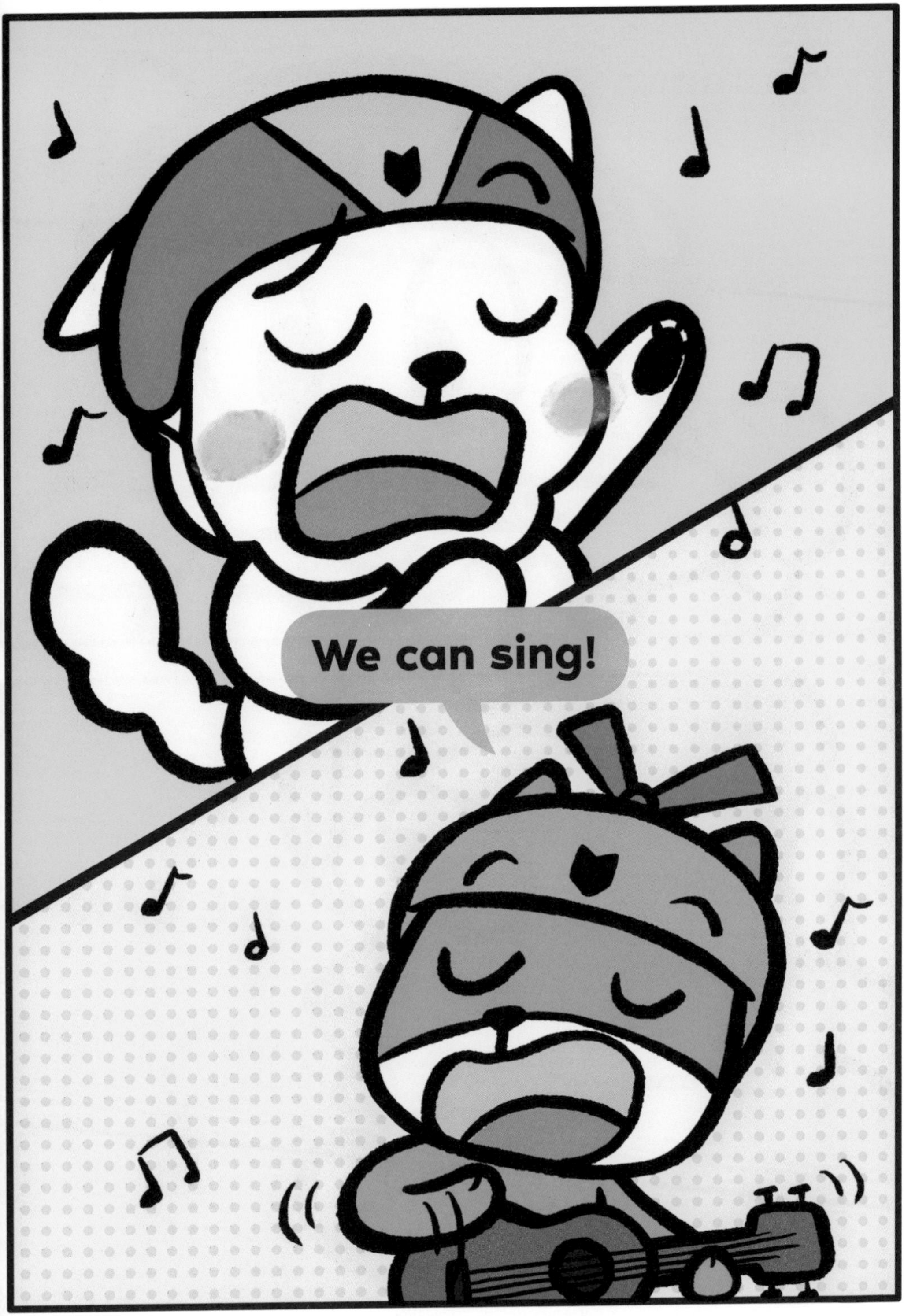
We can sing!

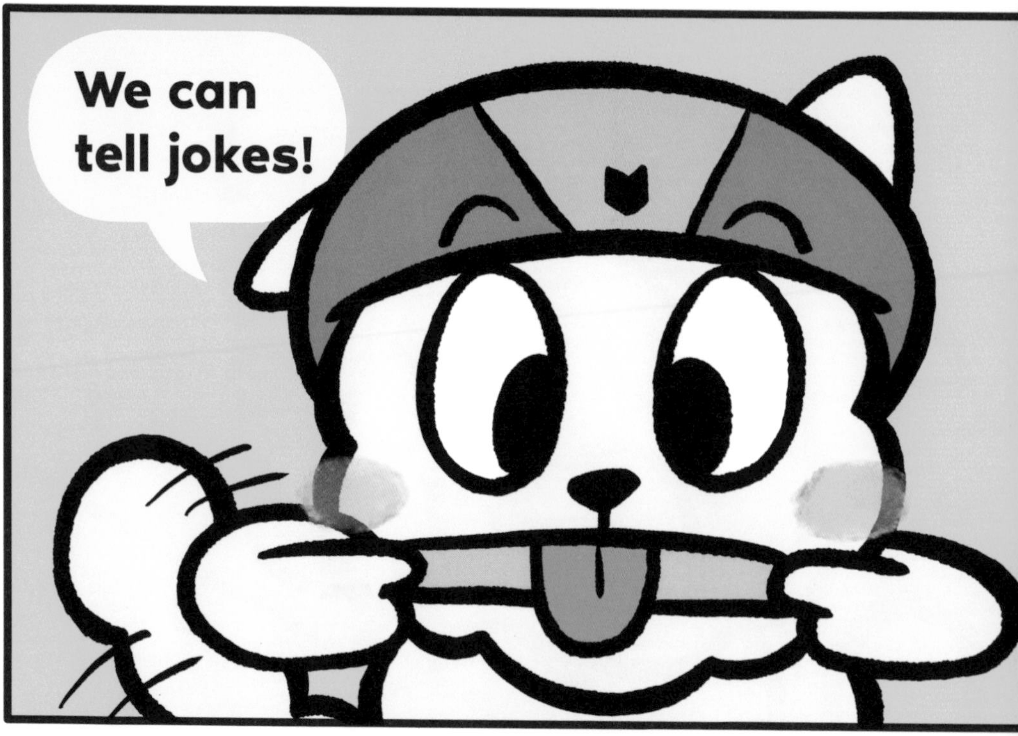
We can tell jokes!

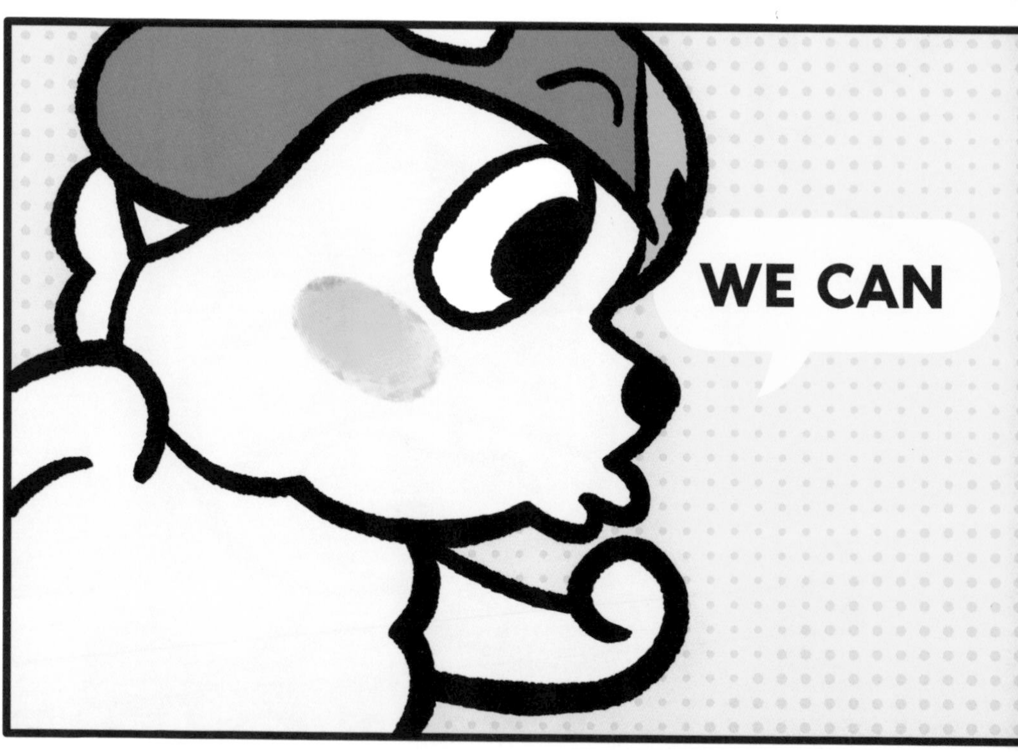
WE CAN

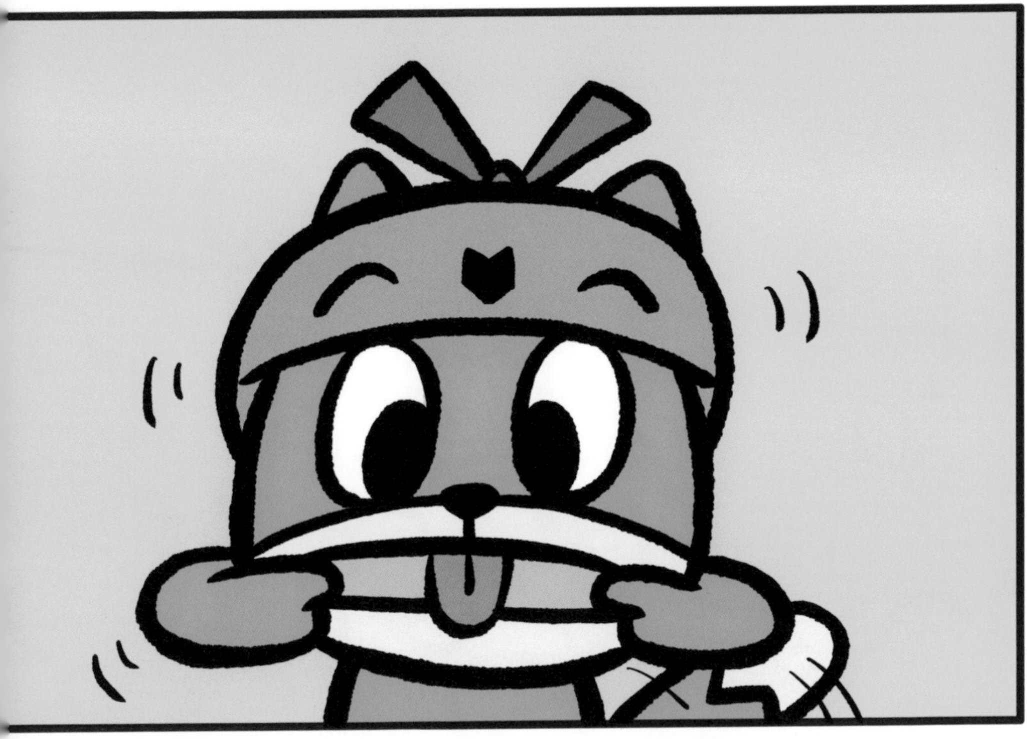

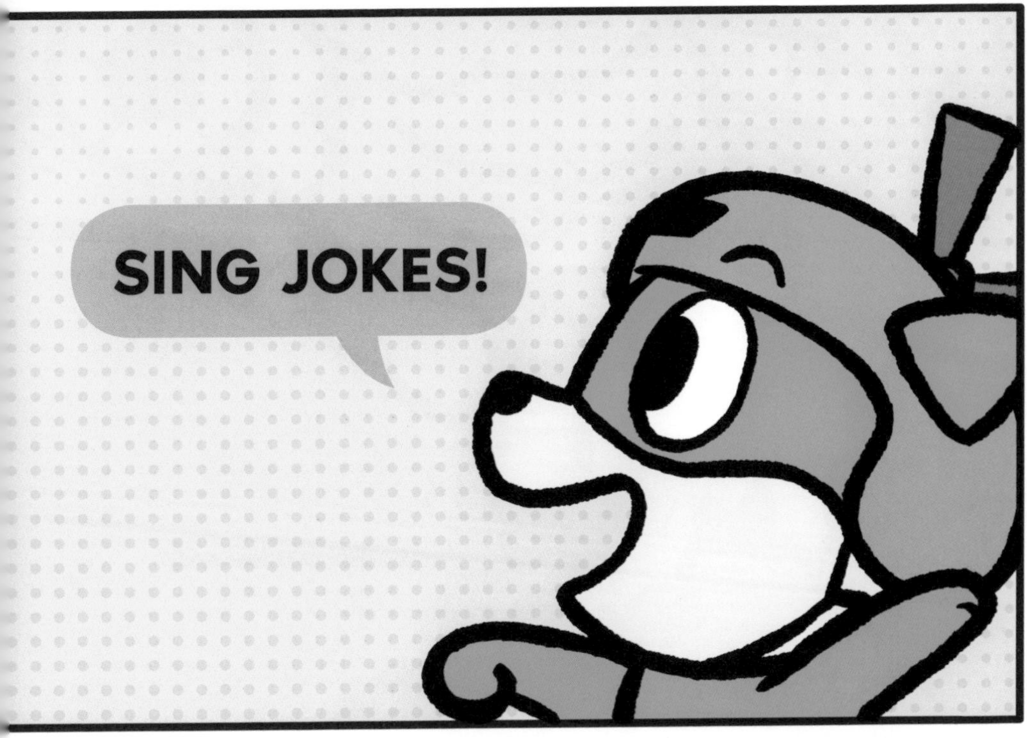
SING JOKES!

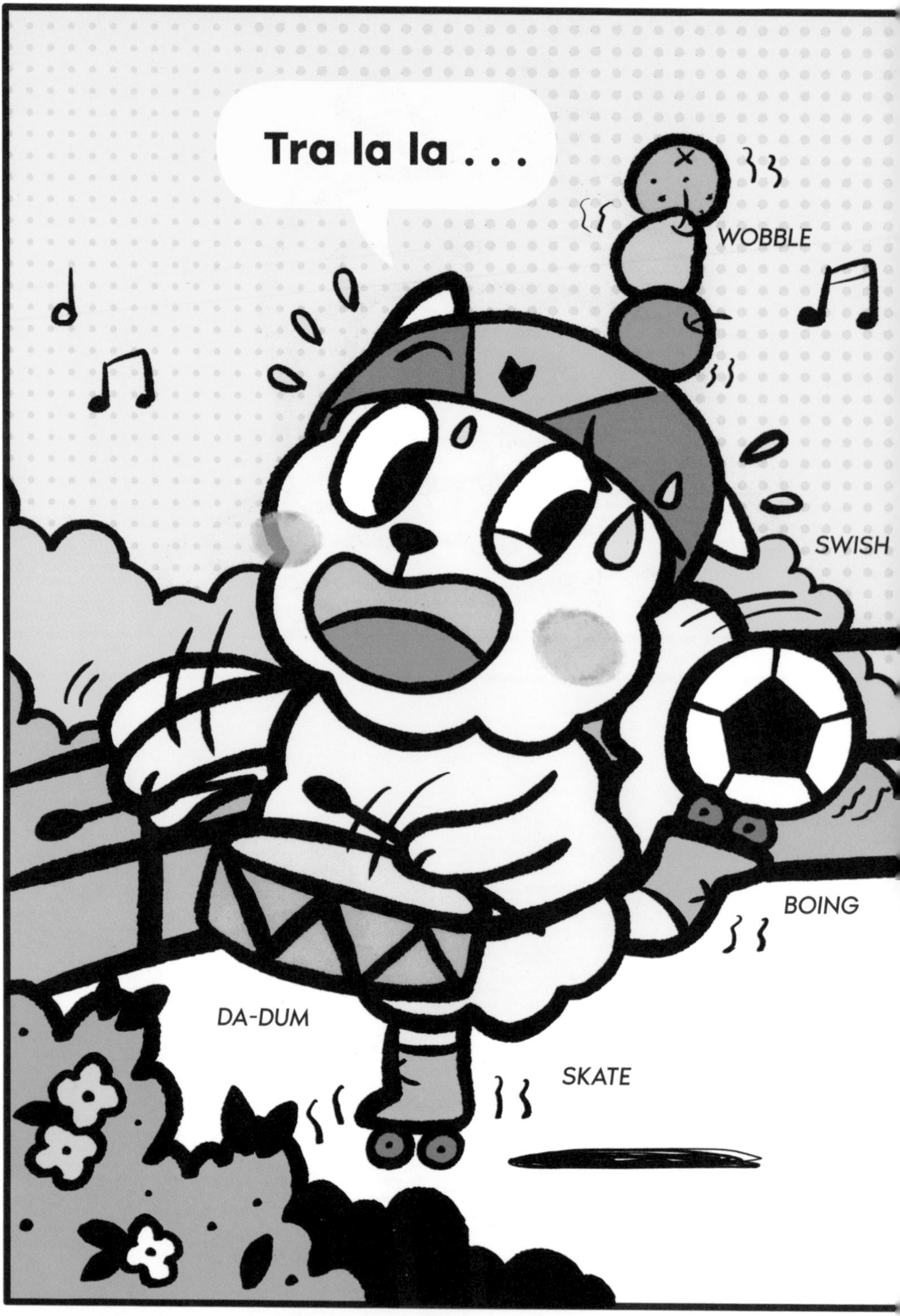
Tra la la . . .
WOBBLE
SWISH
BOING
DA-DUM
SKATE

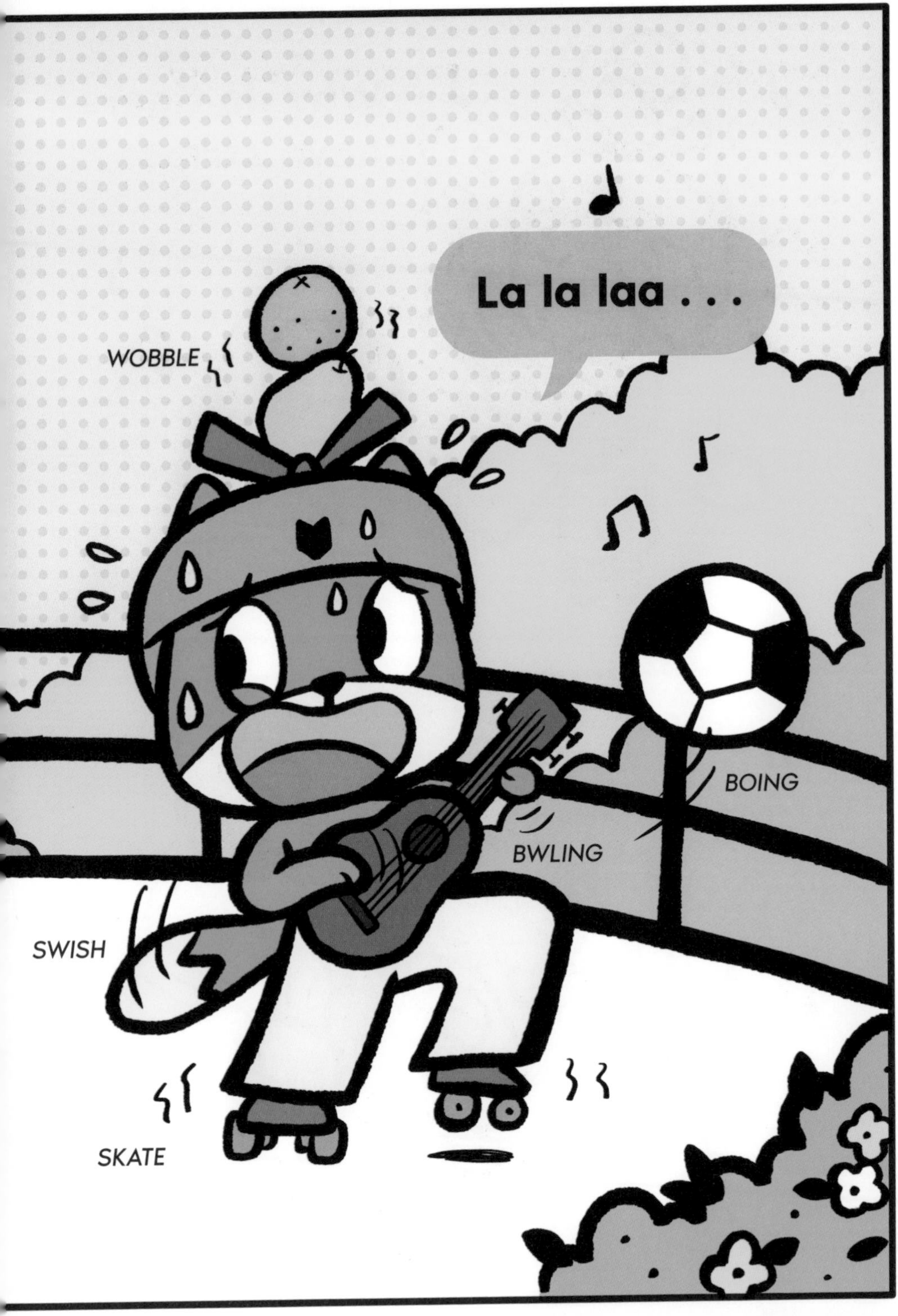
La la laa . . .
WOBBLE
BOING
BWLING
SWISH
SKATE

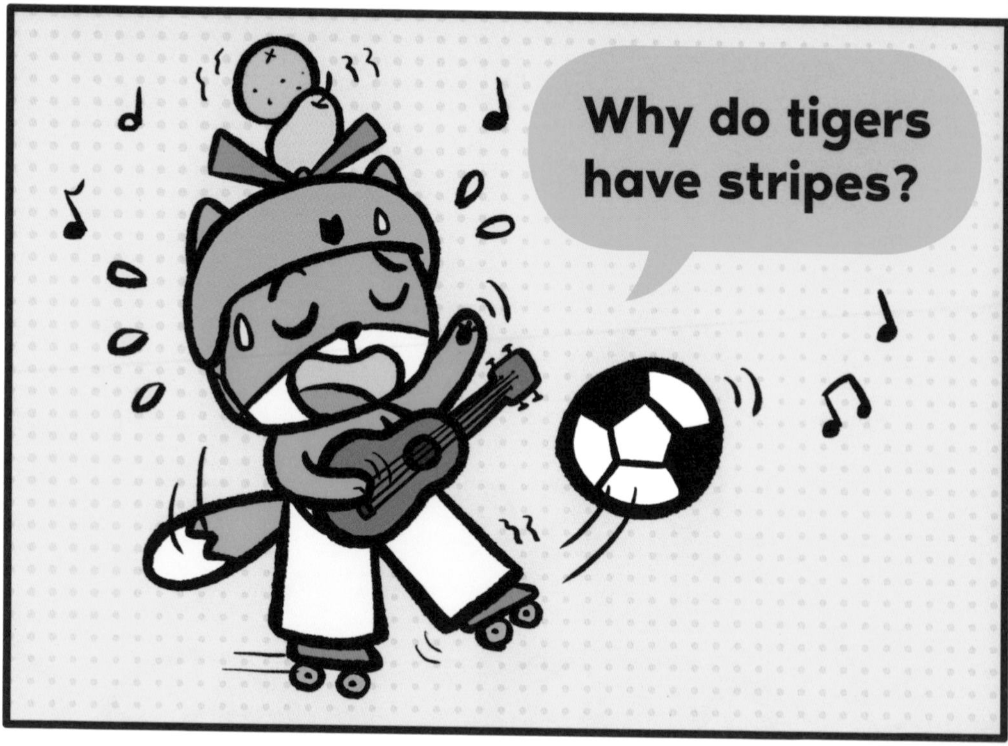
Why do tigers have stripes?

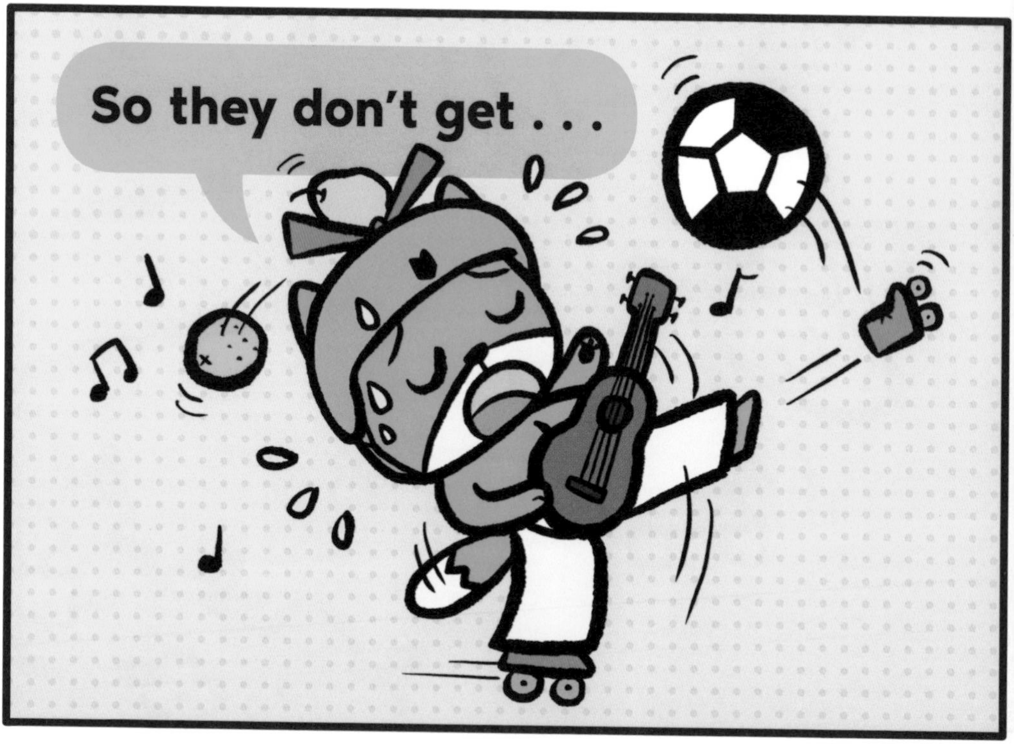
So they don't get . . .

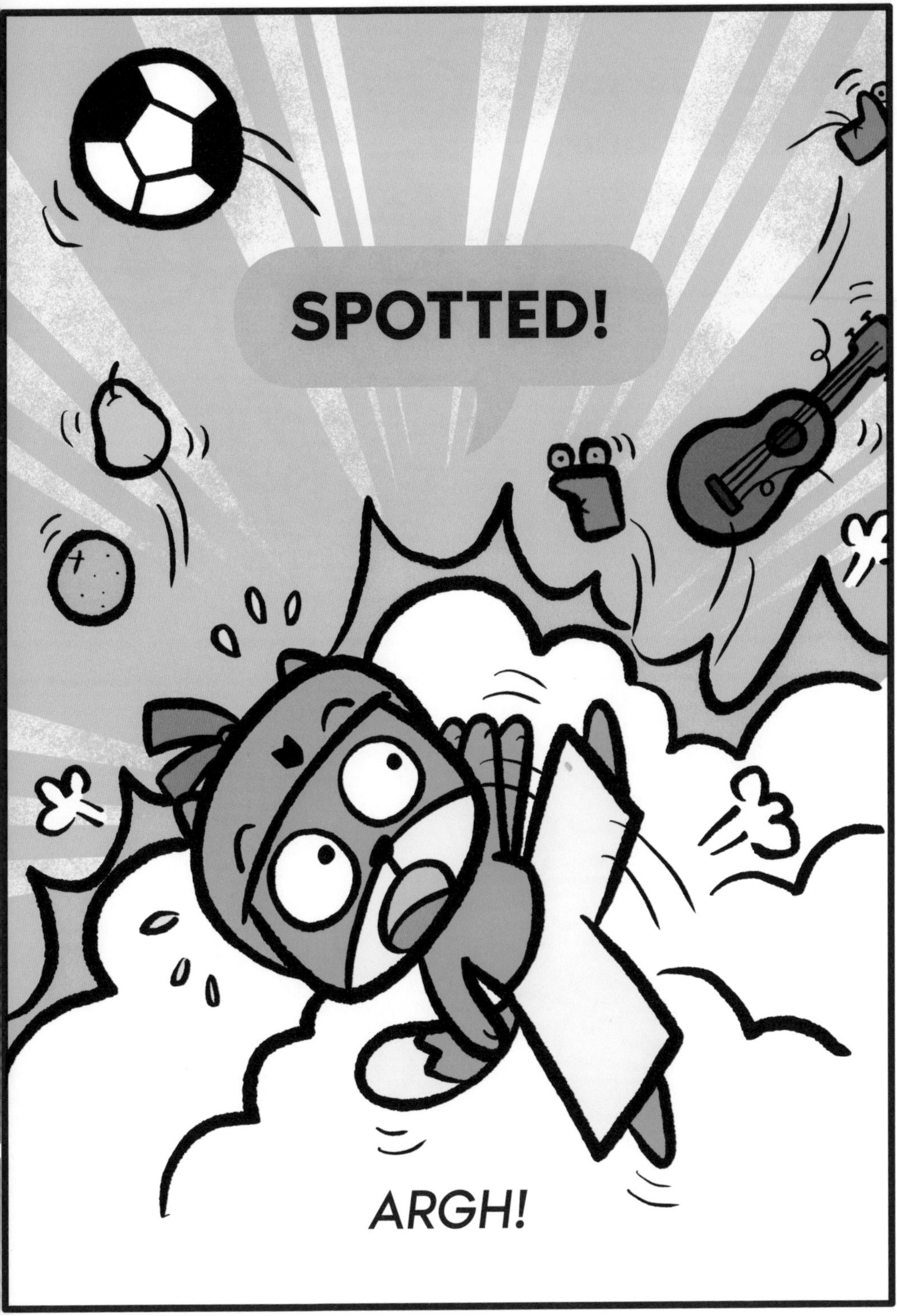
SPOTTED!
ARGH!

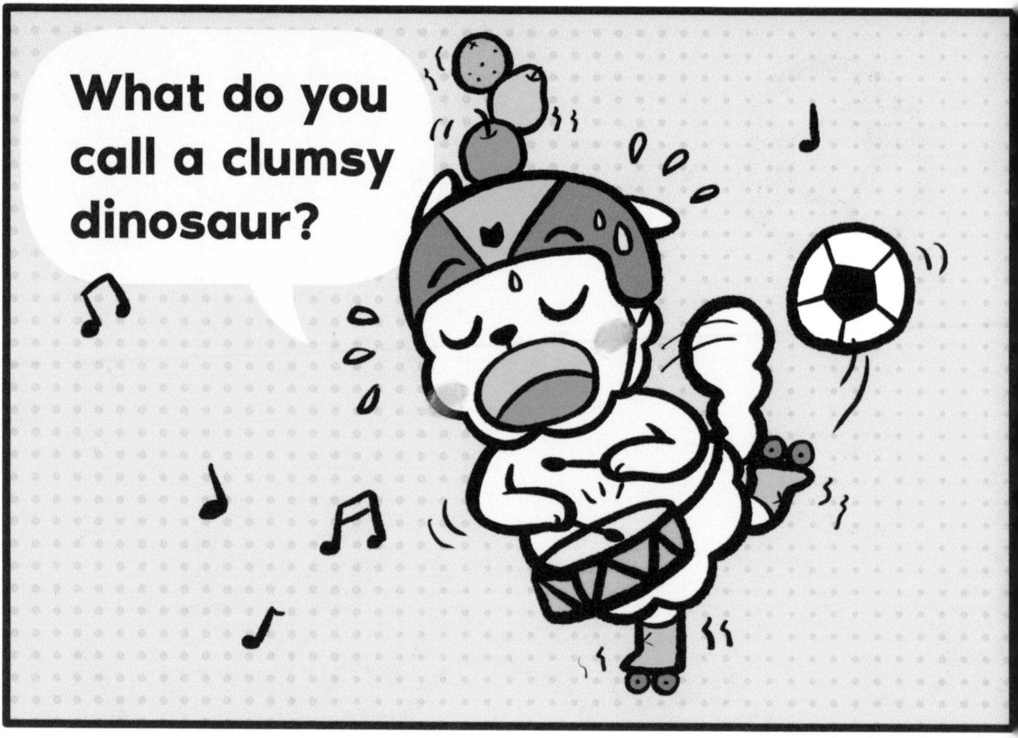
What do you call a clumsy dinosaur?

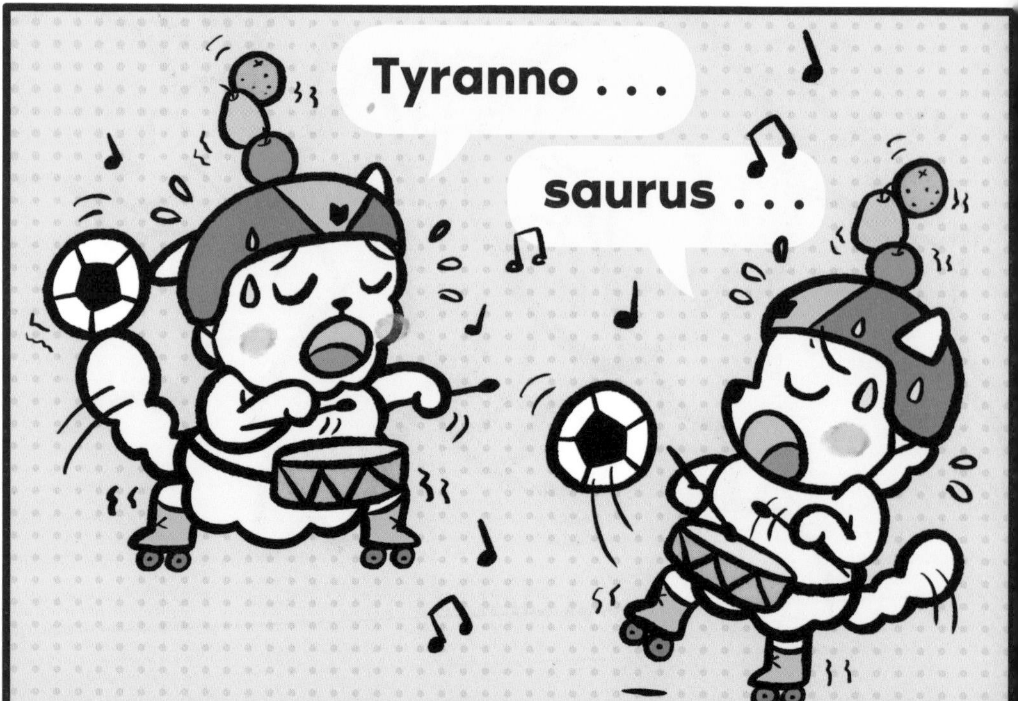
Tyranno . . .
saurus . . .

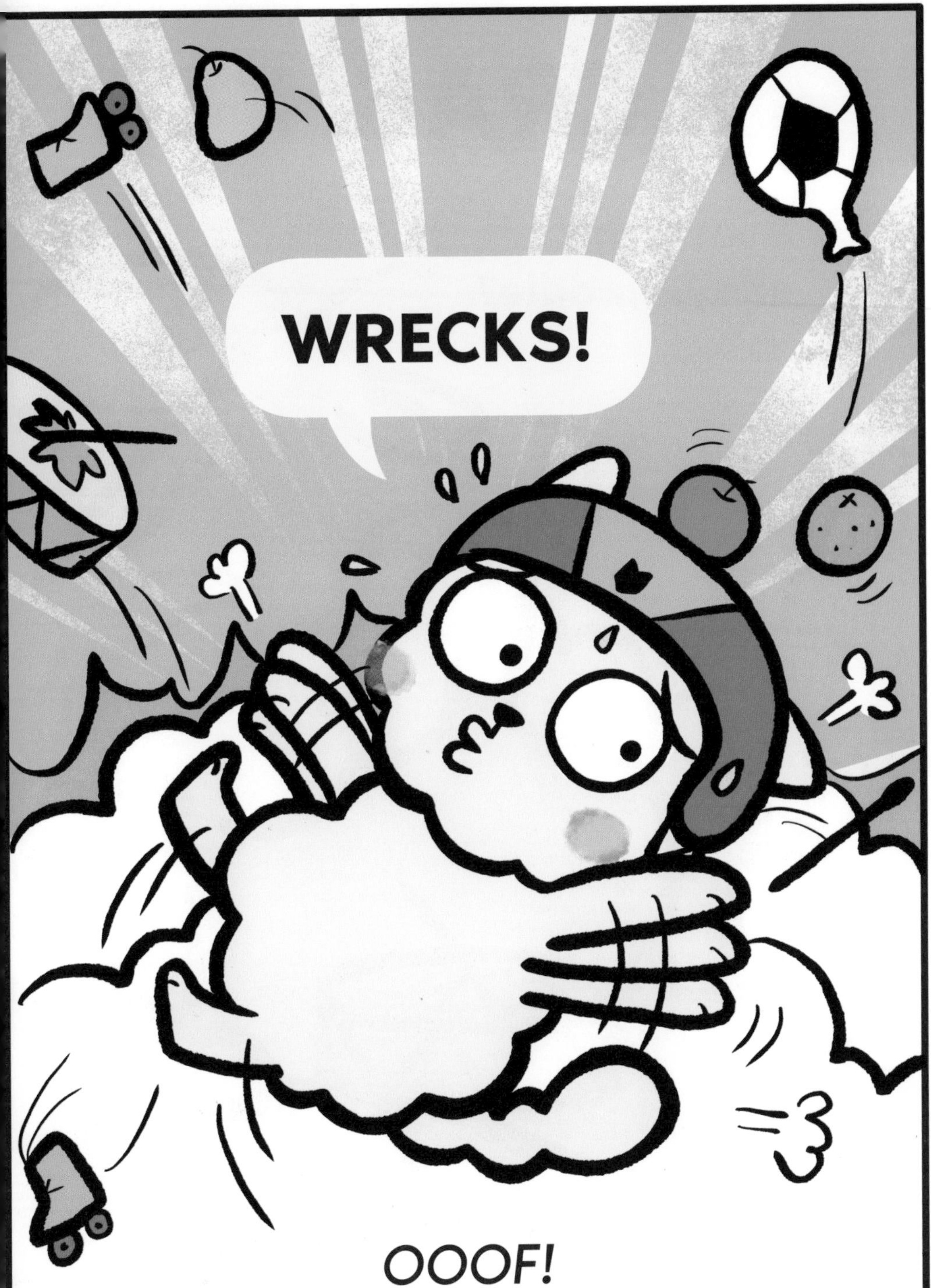
WRECKS!
OOOF!

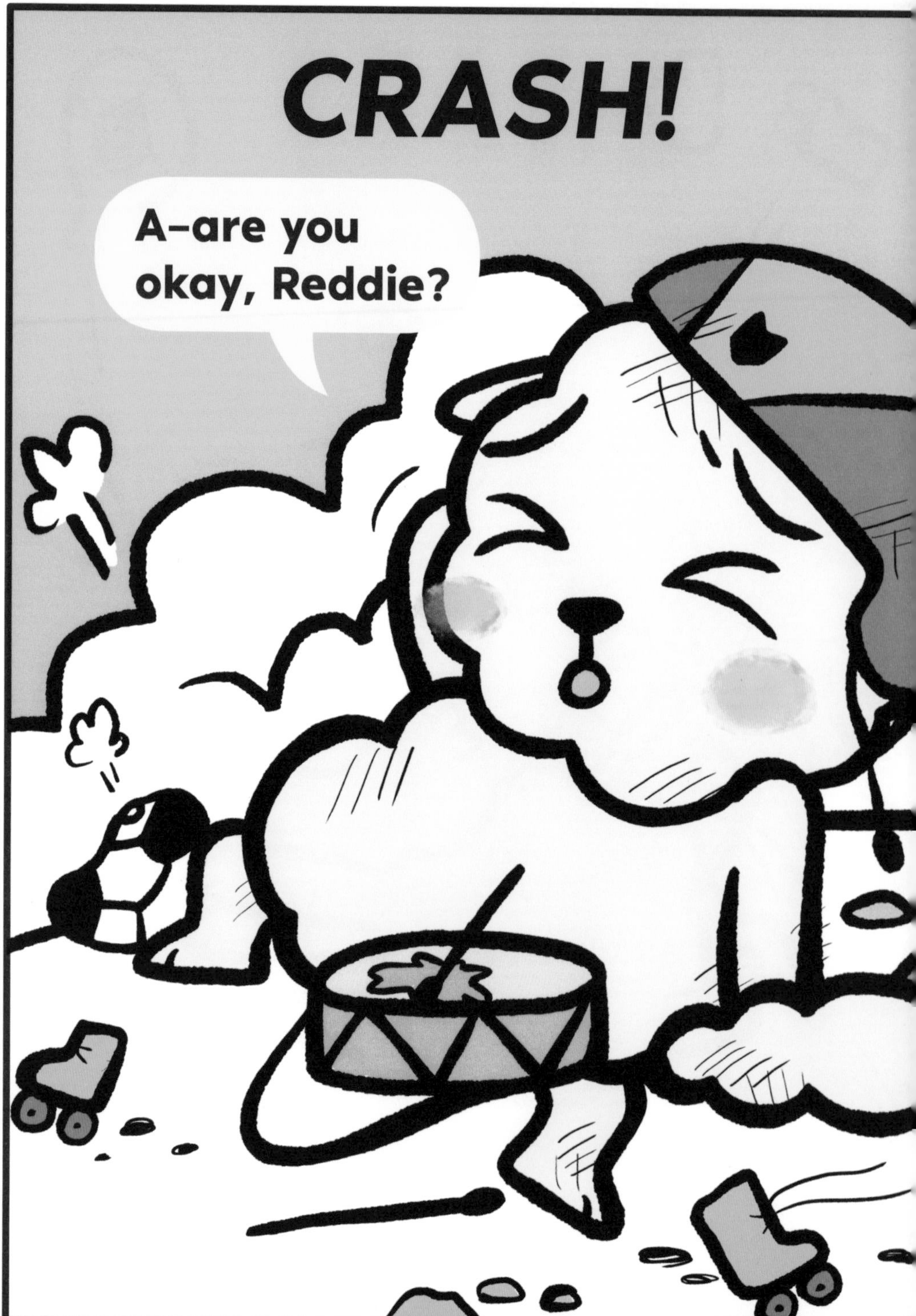
CRASH!
A-are you okay, Reddie?

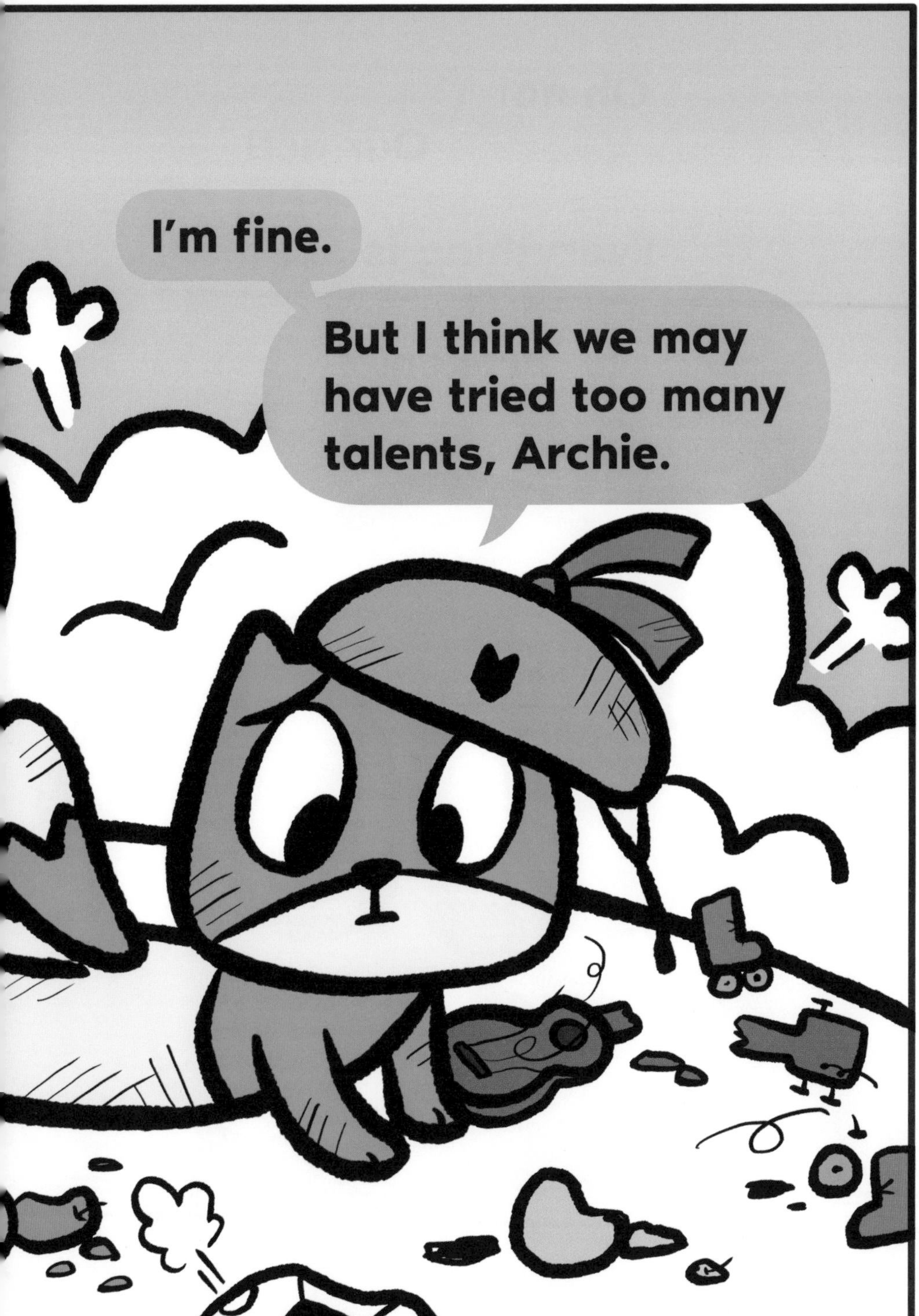
I'm fine.
But I think we may have tried too many talents, Archie.

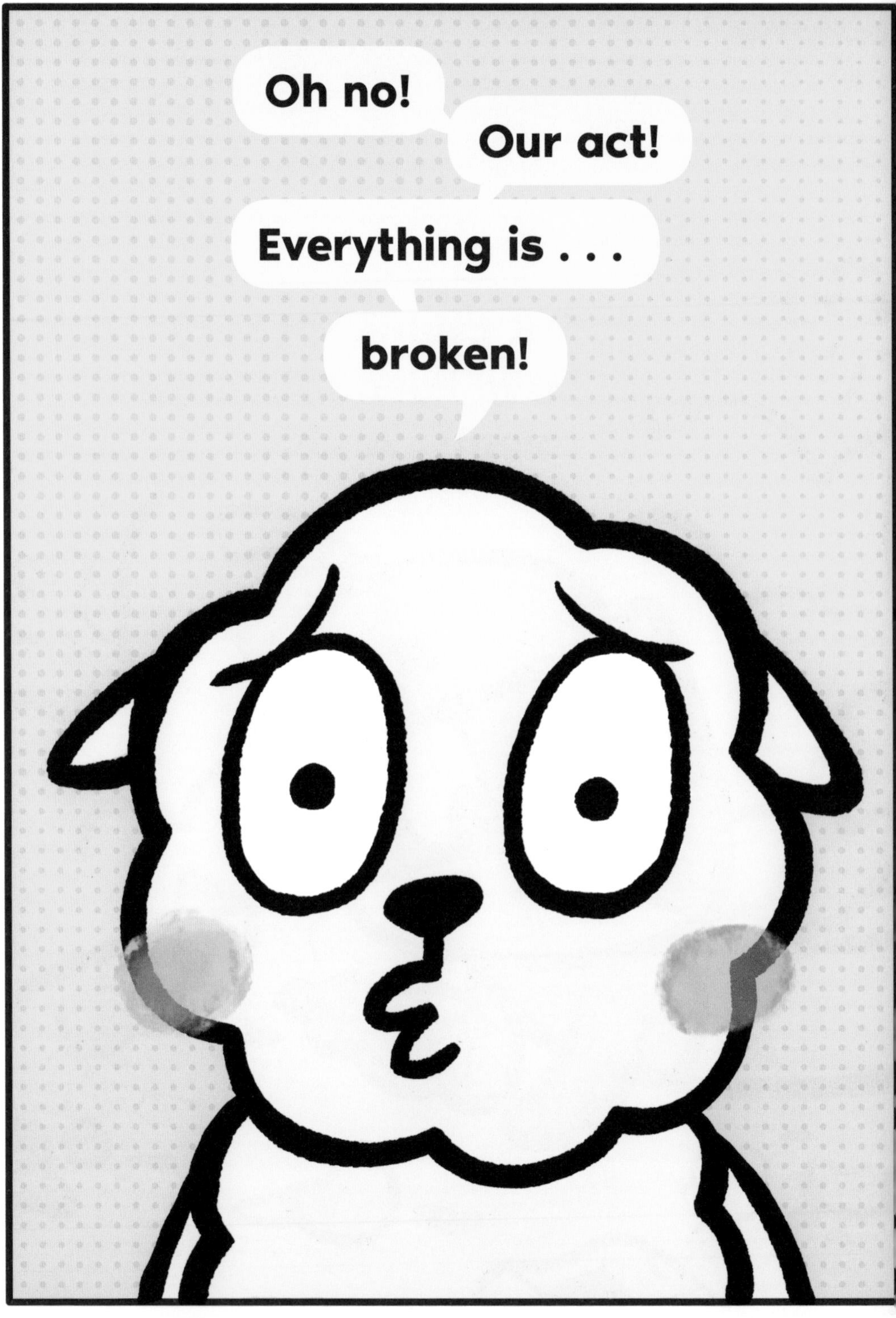

Oh no!
Our act!
Everything is . . .
broken!

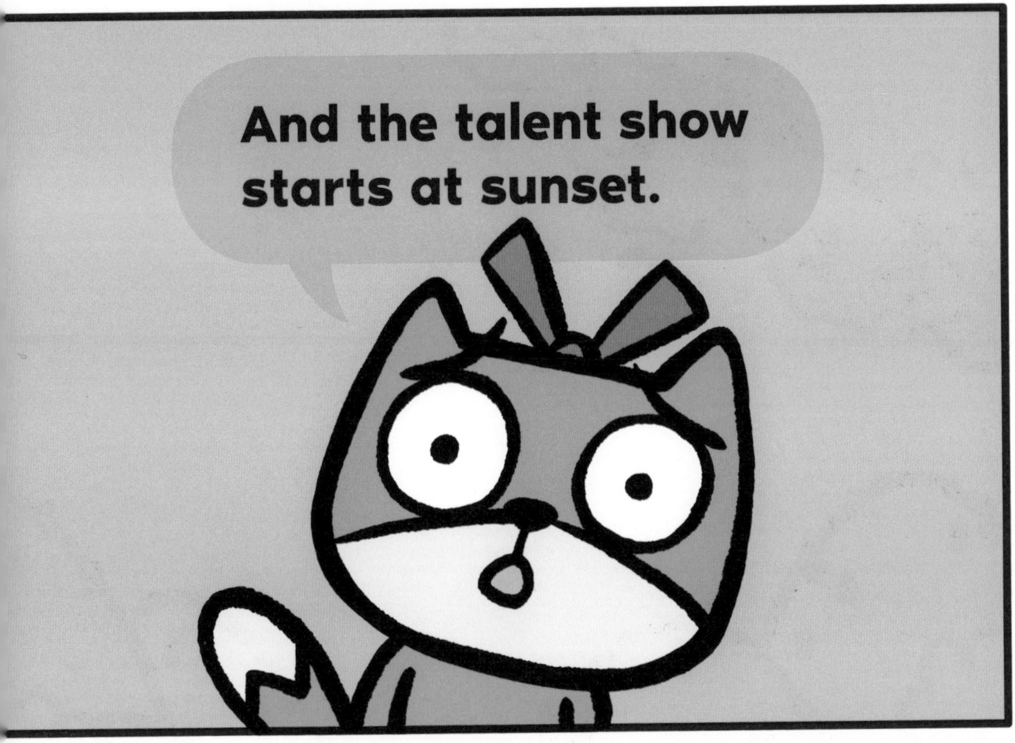
And the talent show starts at sunset.

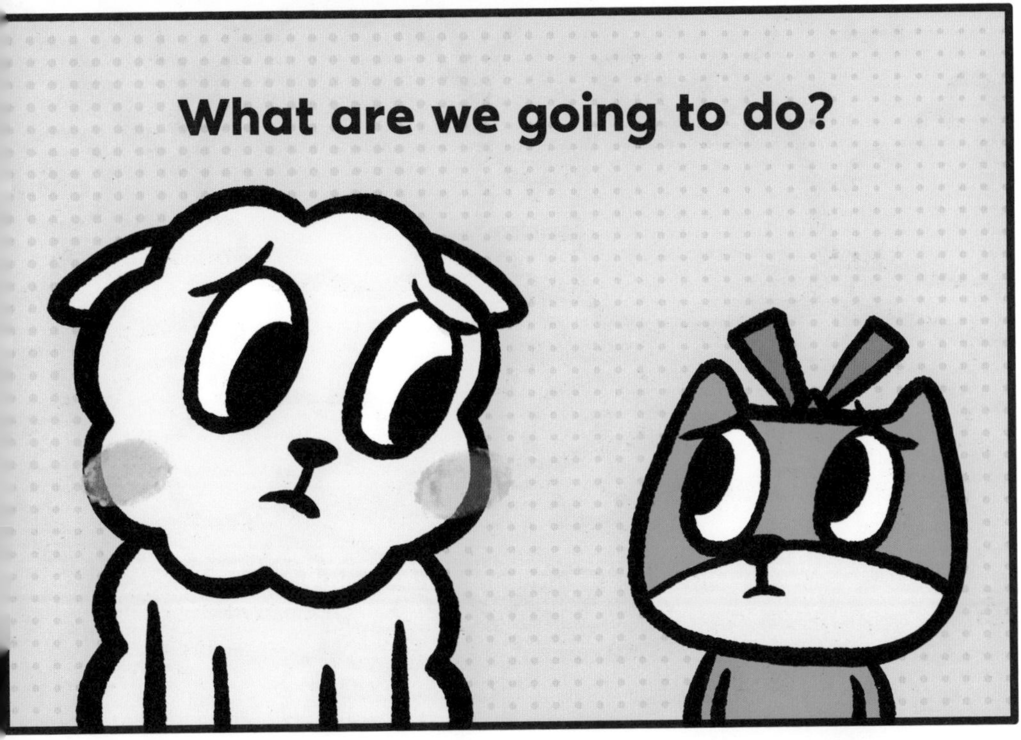
What are we going to do?

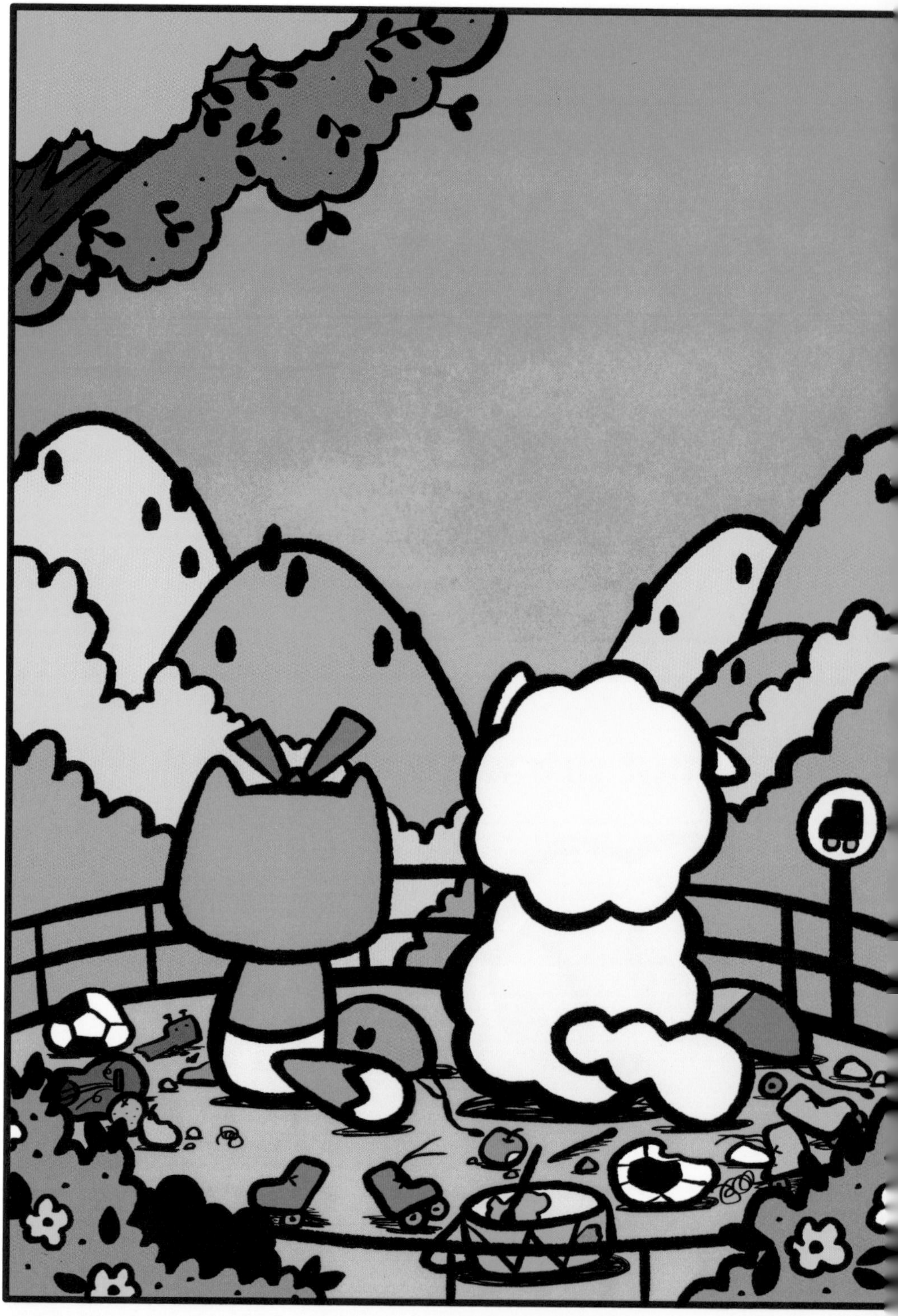

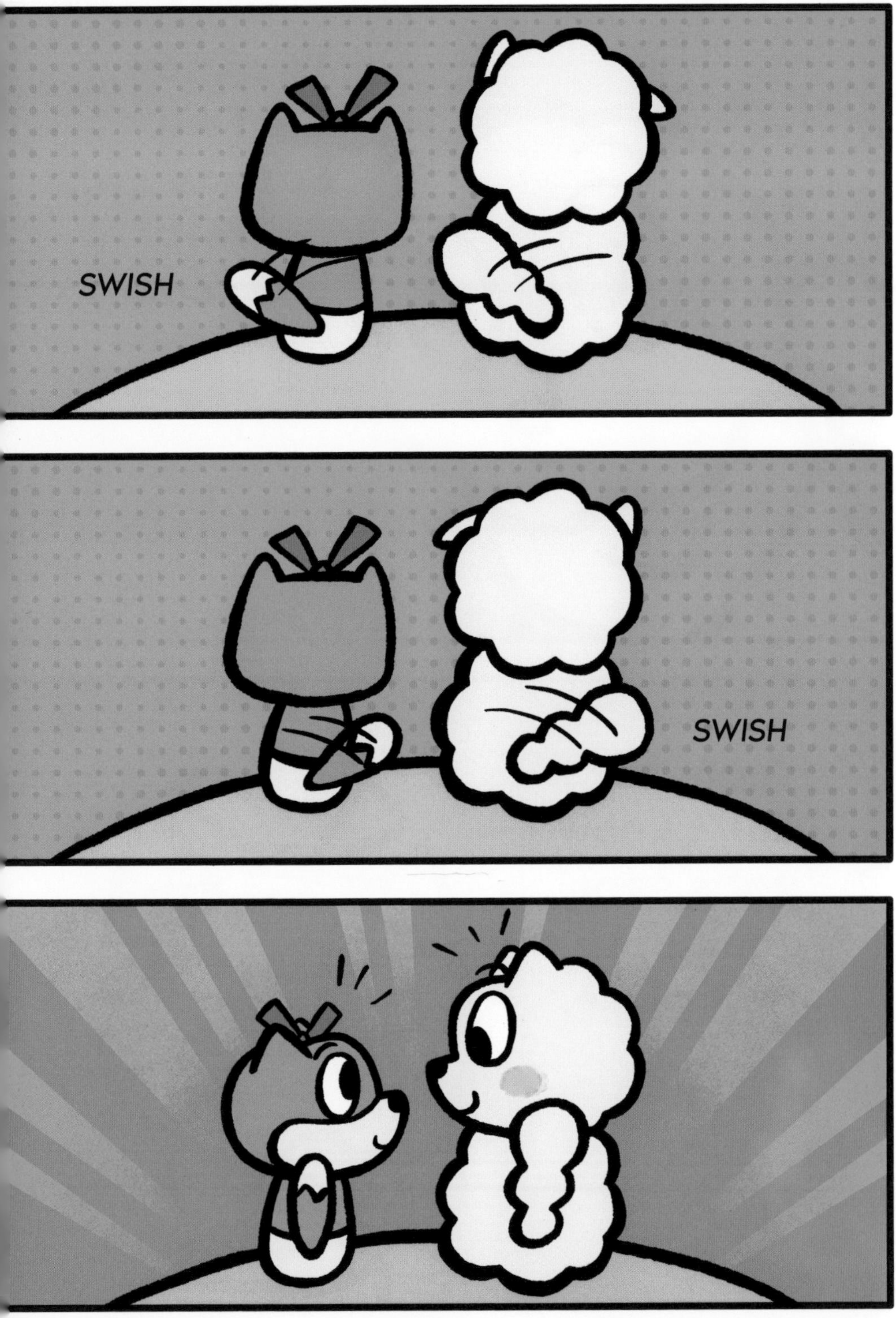
SWISH
SWISH

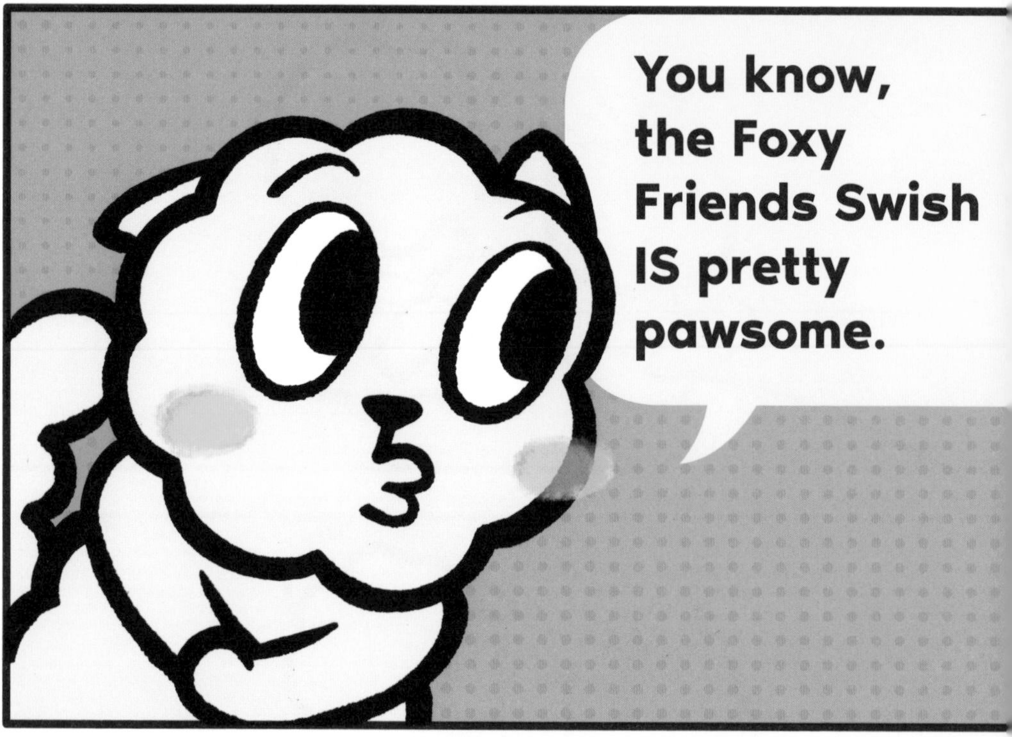
You know, the Foxy Friends Swish IS pretty pawsome.

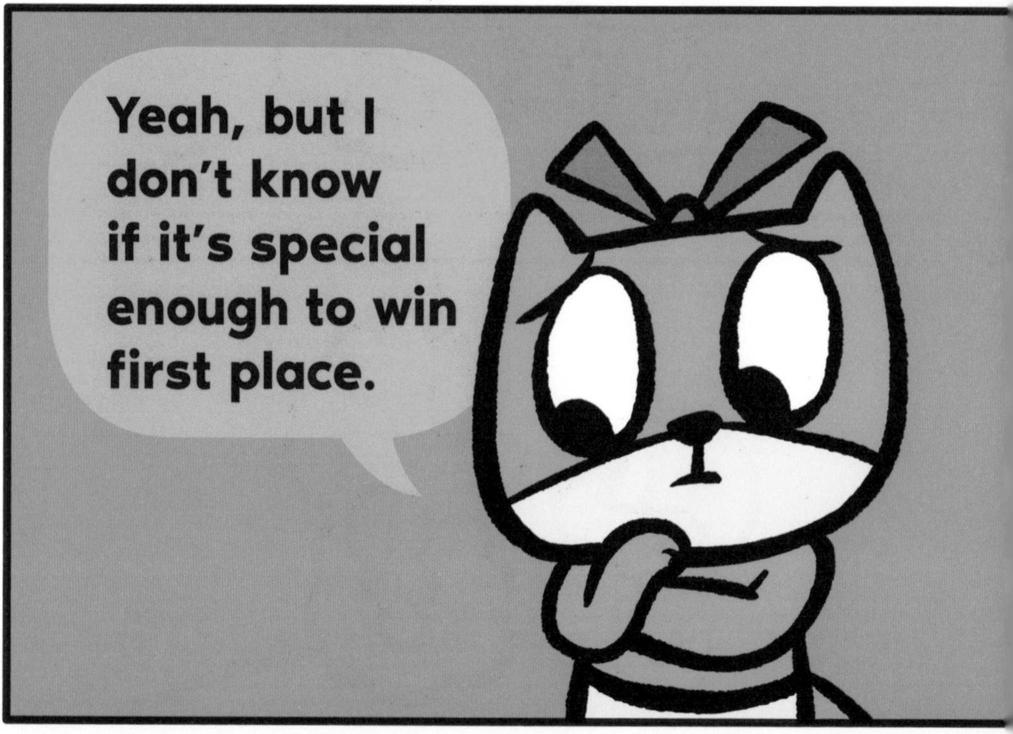
Yeah, but I don't know if it's special enough to win first place.

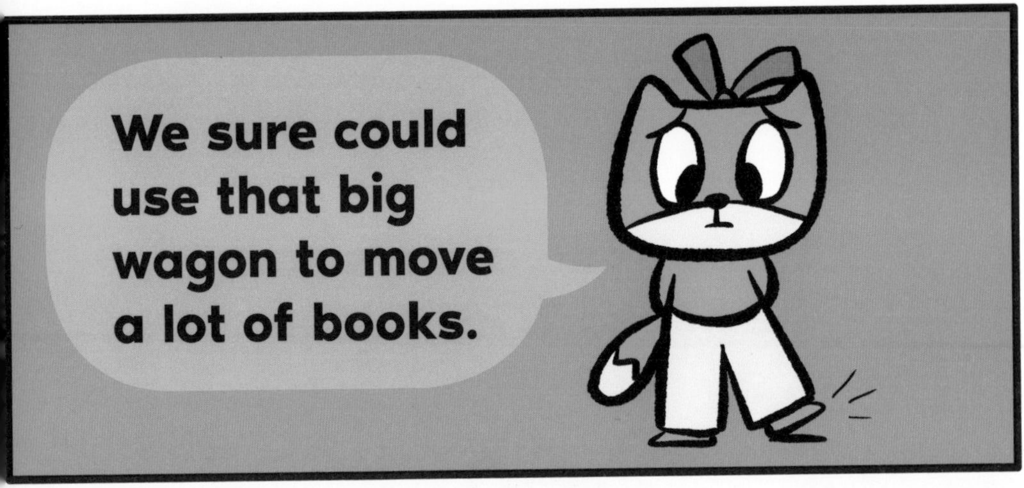
We sure could use that big wagon to move a lot of books.

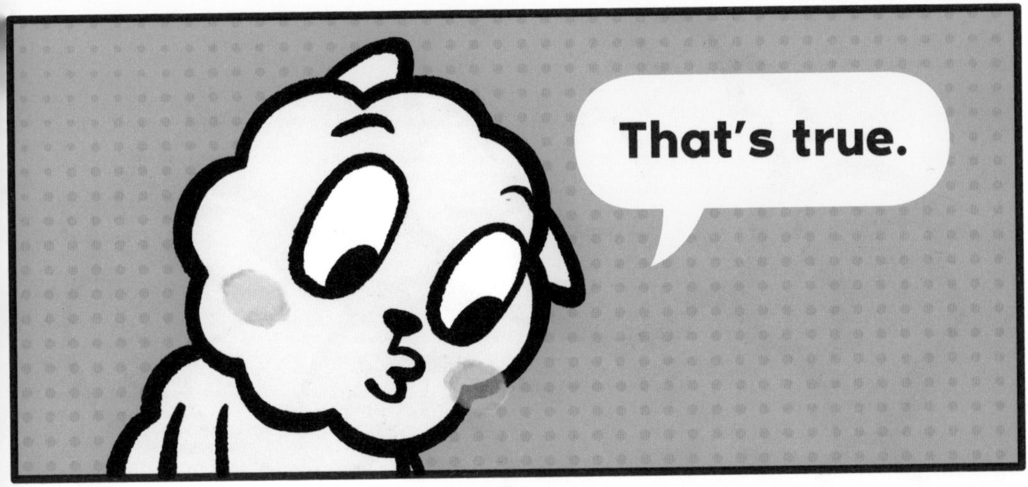
That's true.

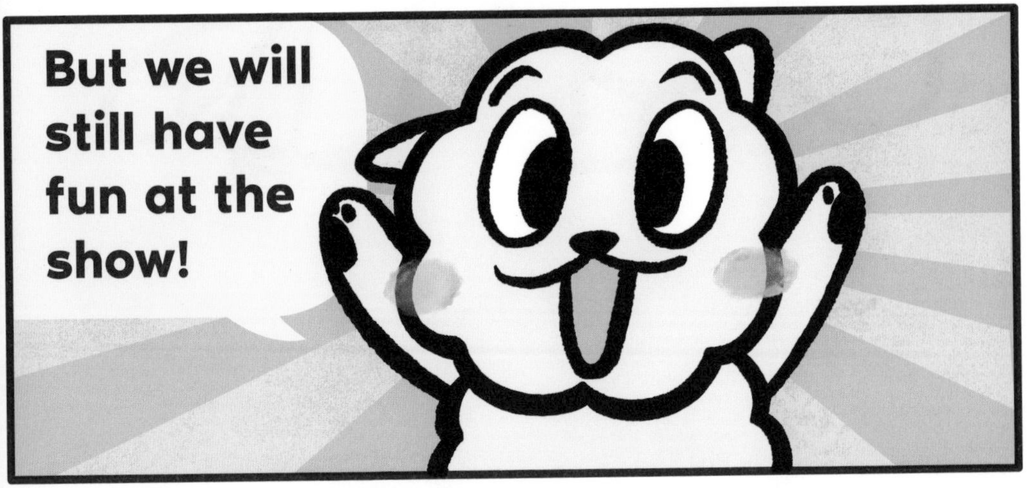
But we will still have fun at the show!

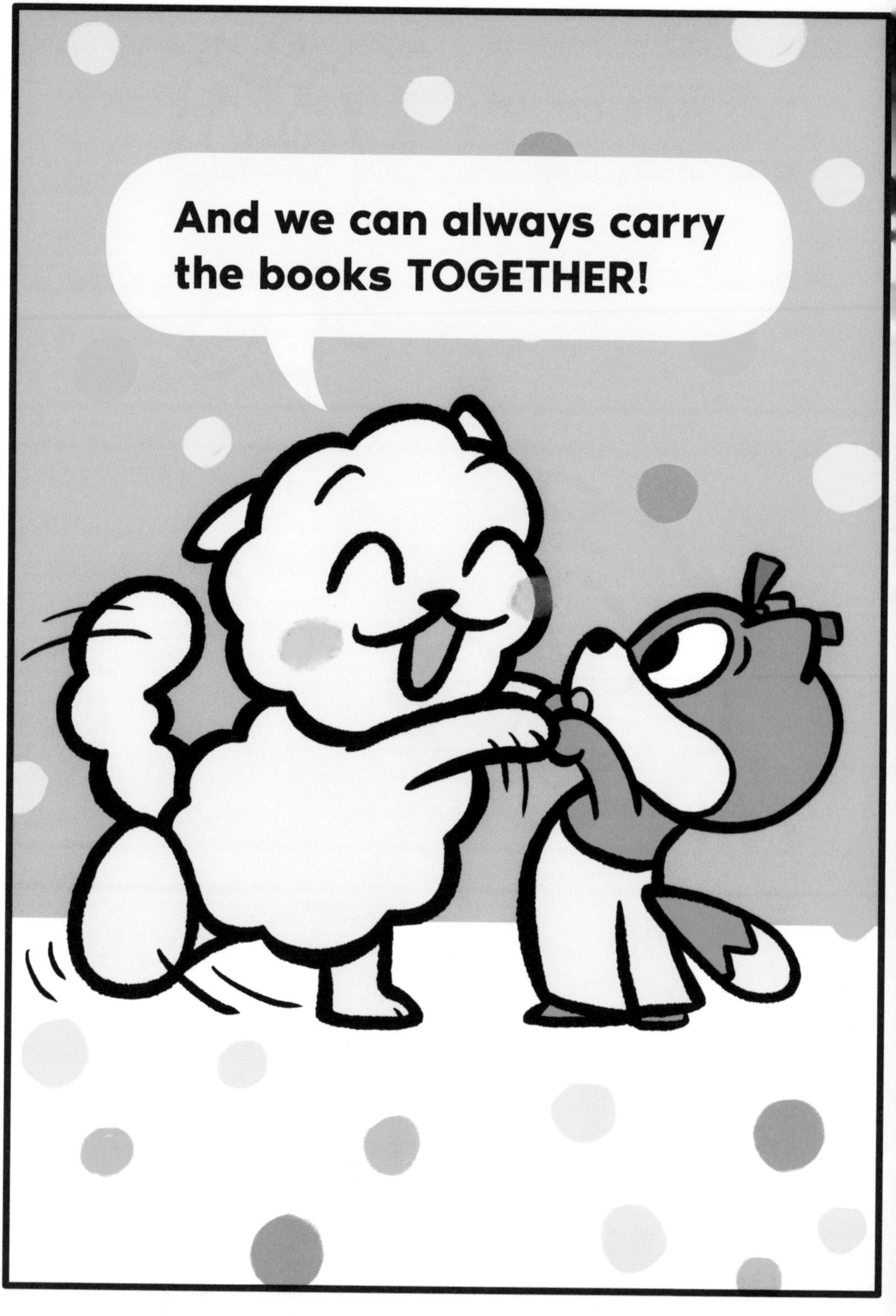
And we can always carry the books TOGETHER!

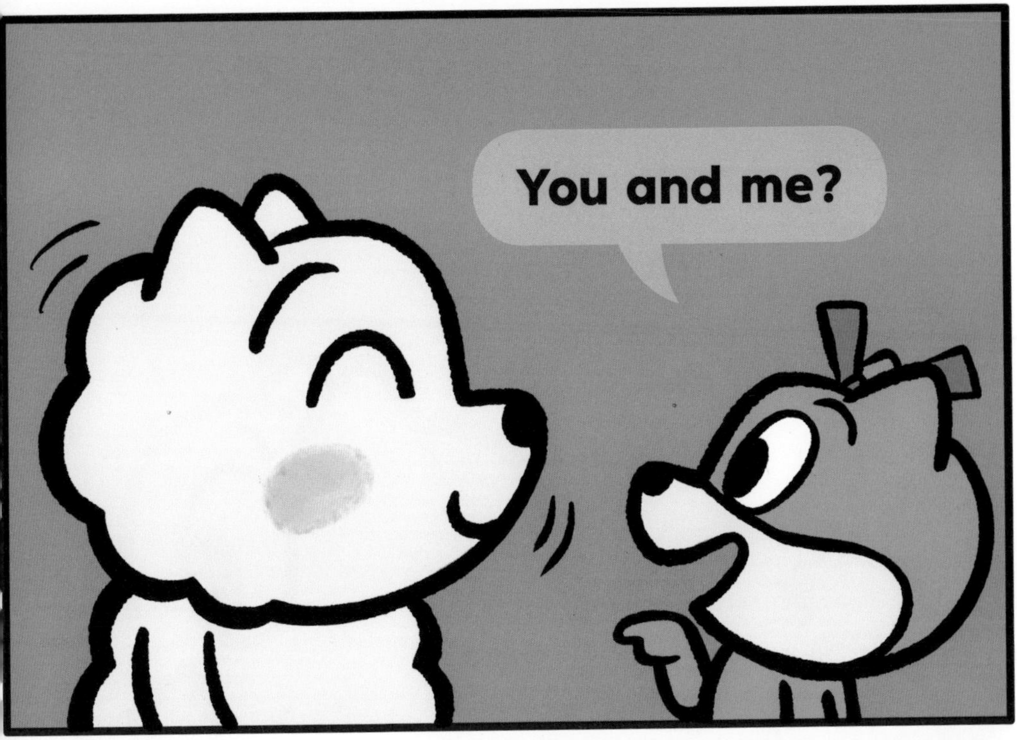
You and me?

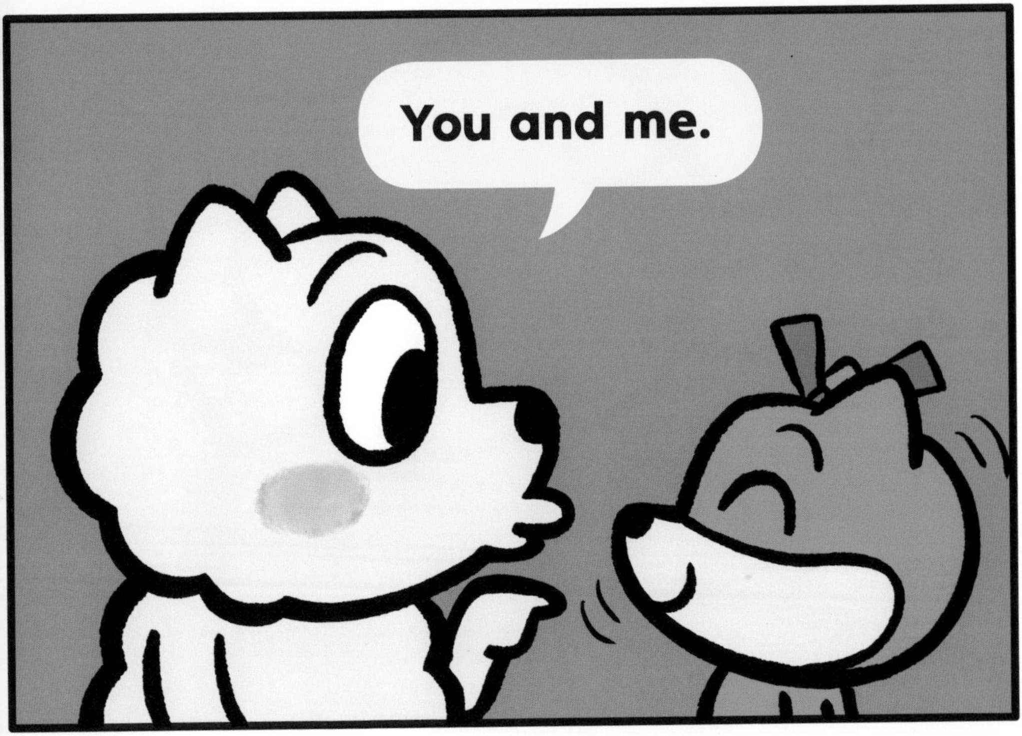
You and me.

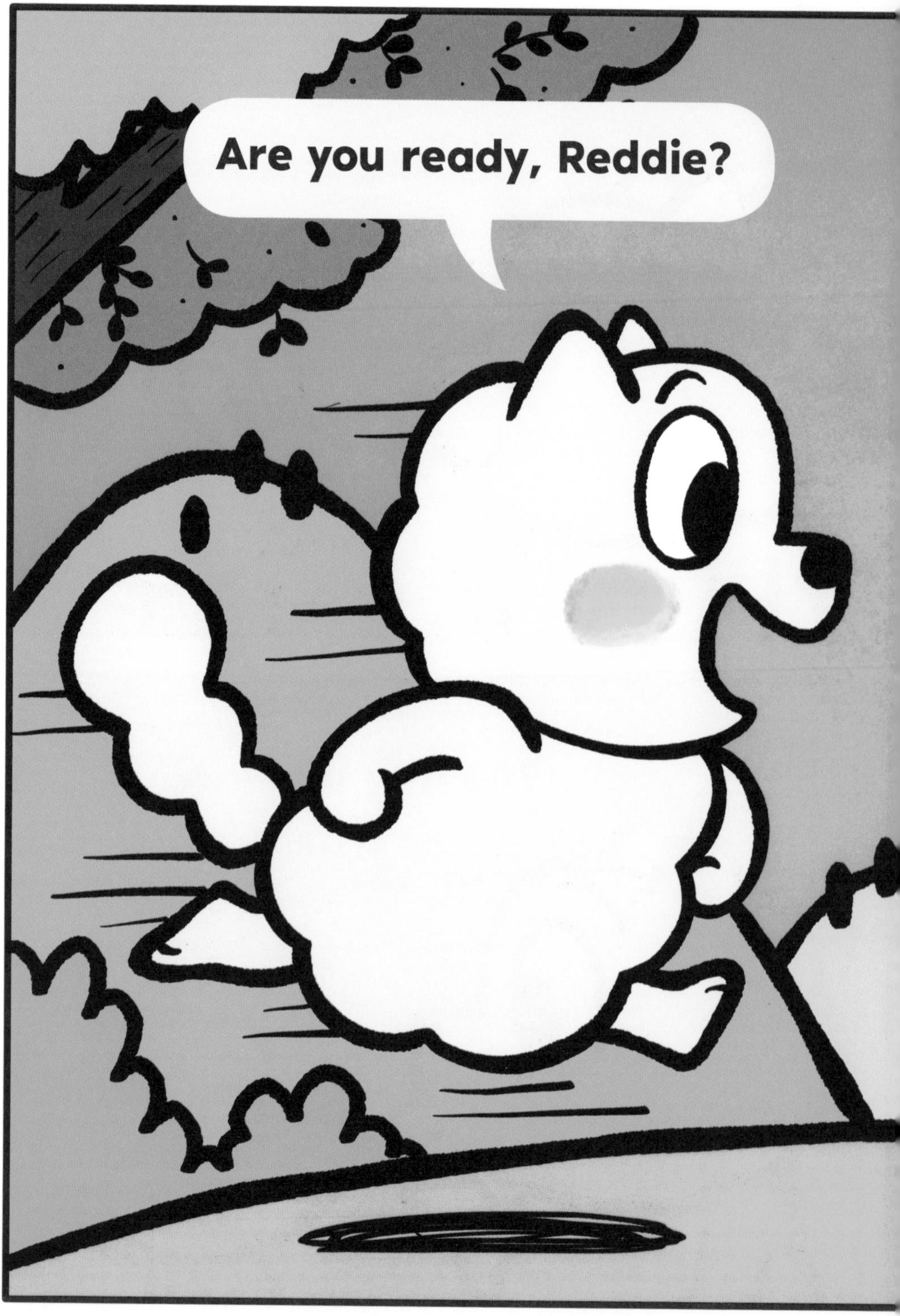
Are you ready, Reddie?

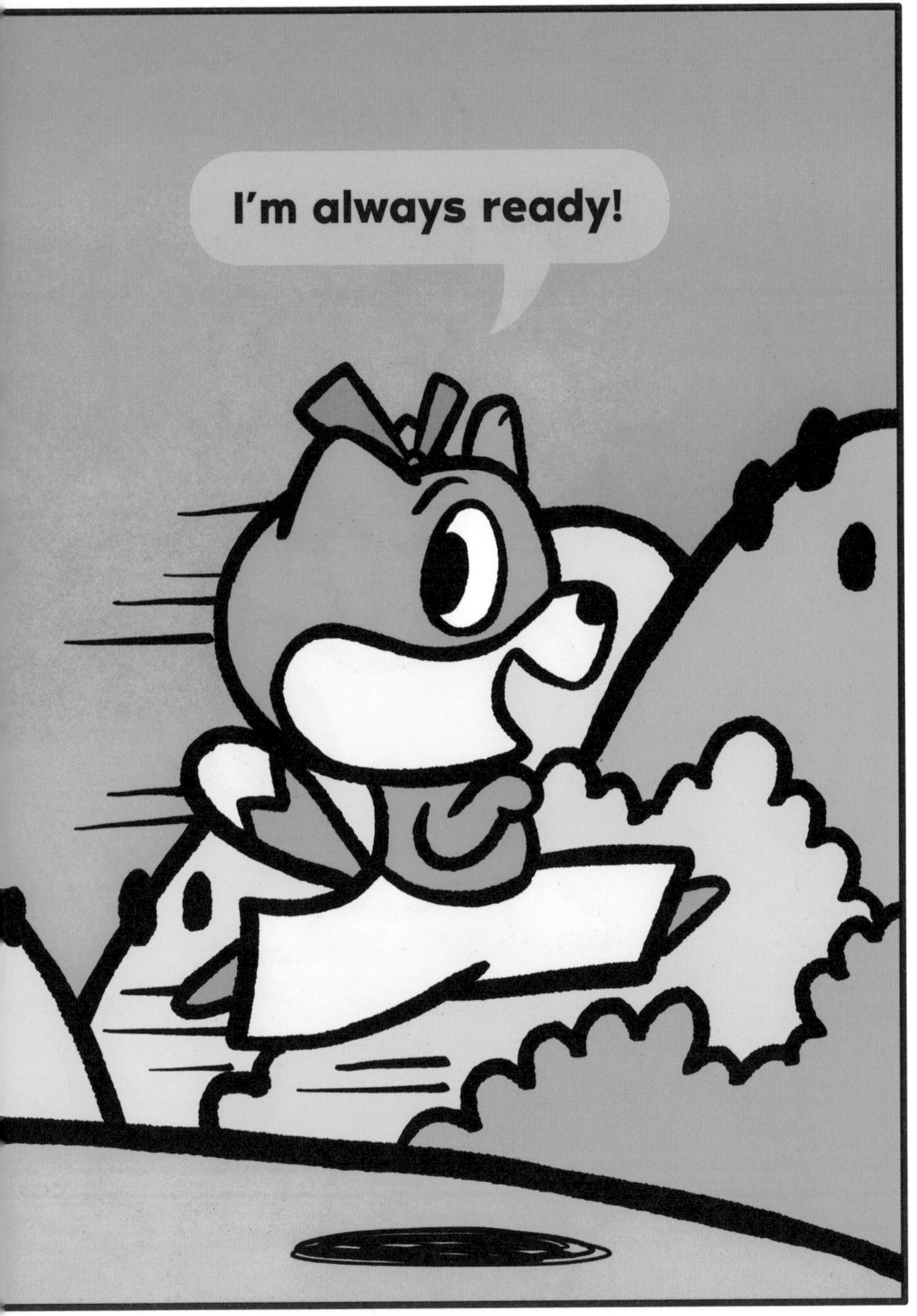
I'm always ready!

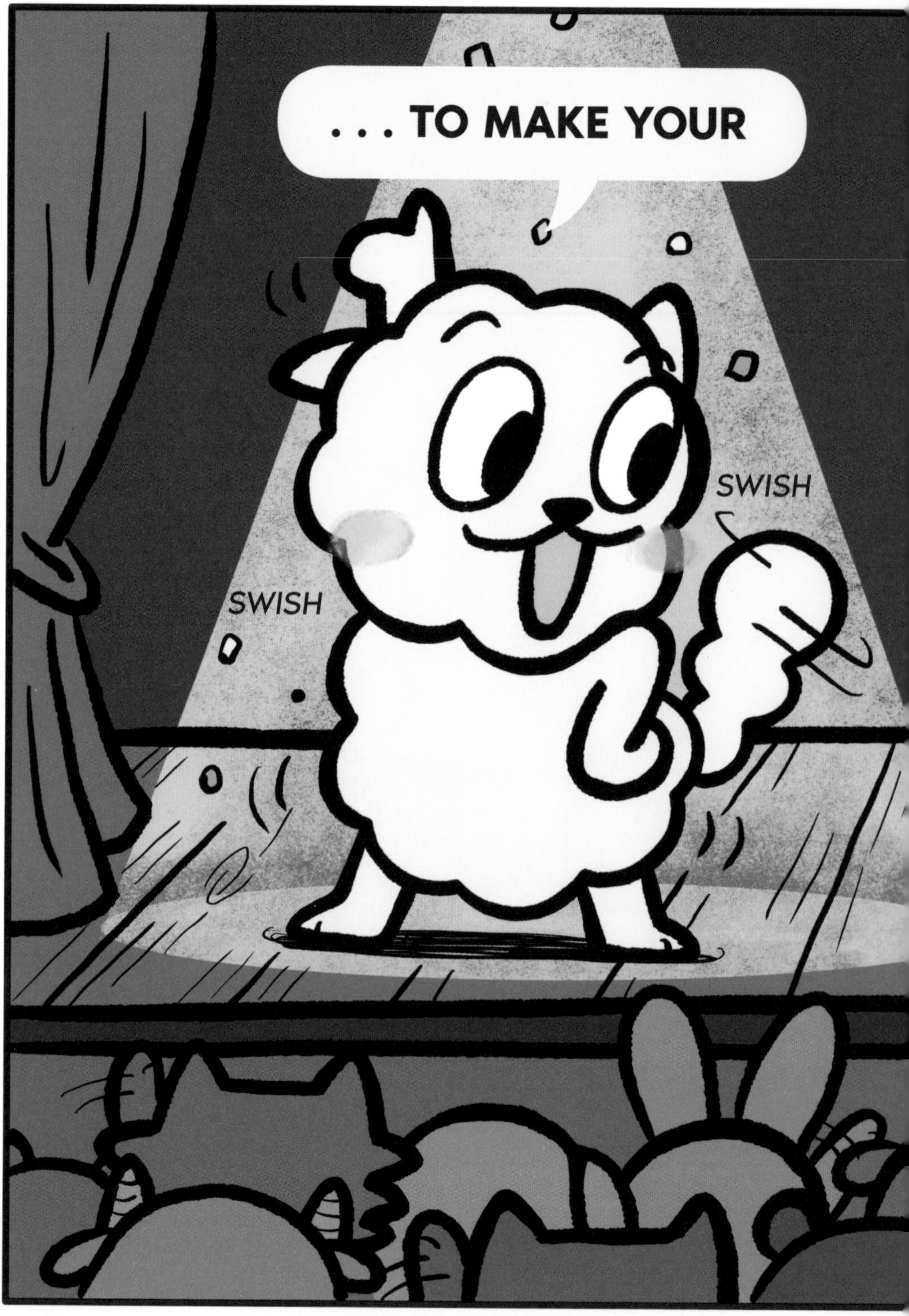

. . . TO MAKE YOUR
SWISH
SWISH

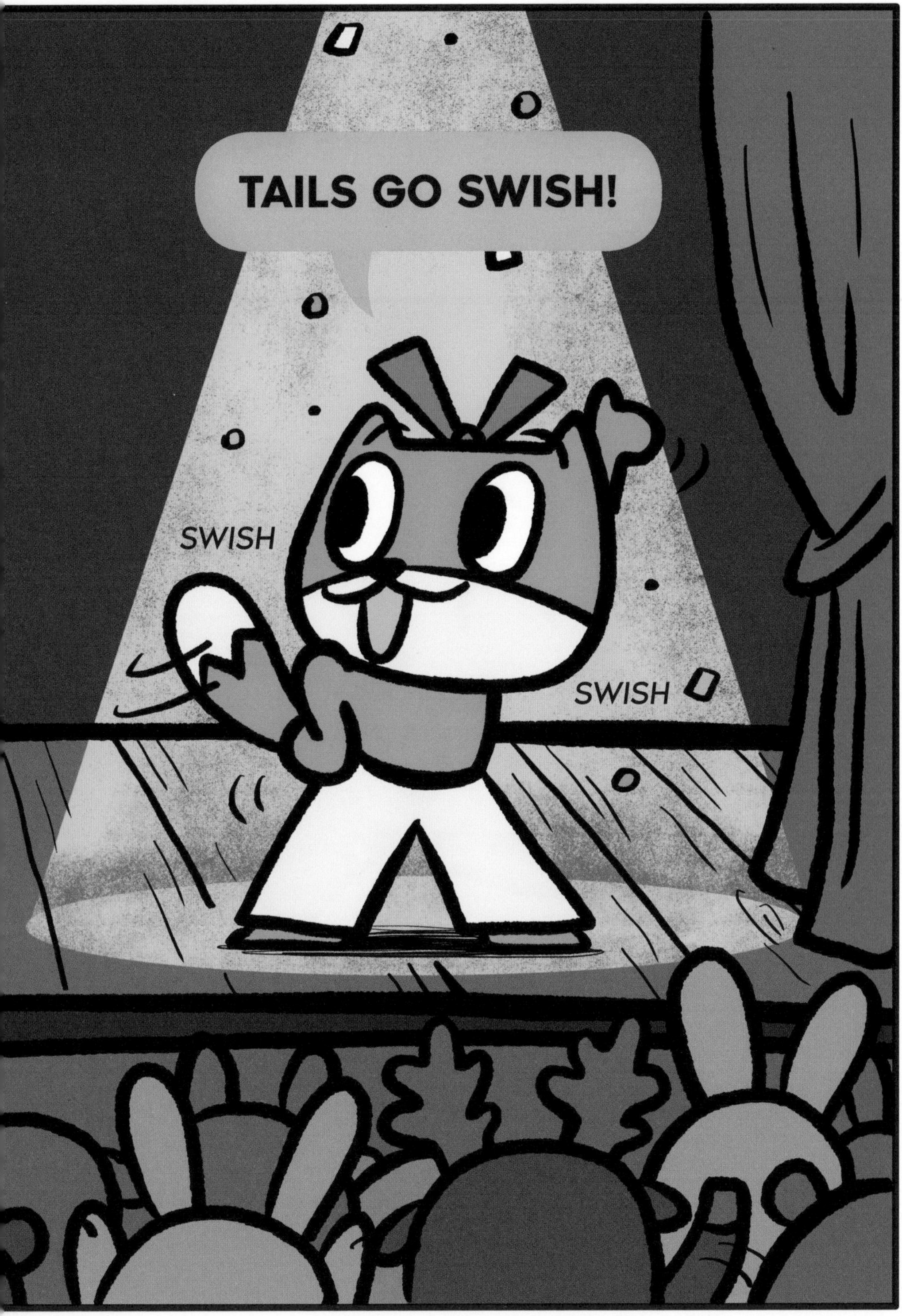
TAILS GO SWISH!
SWISH
SWISH

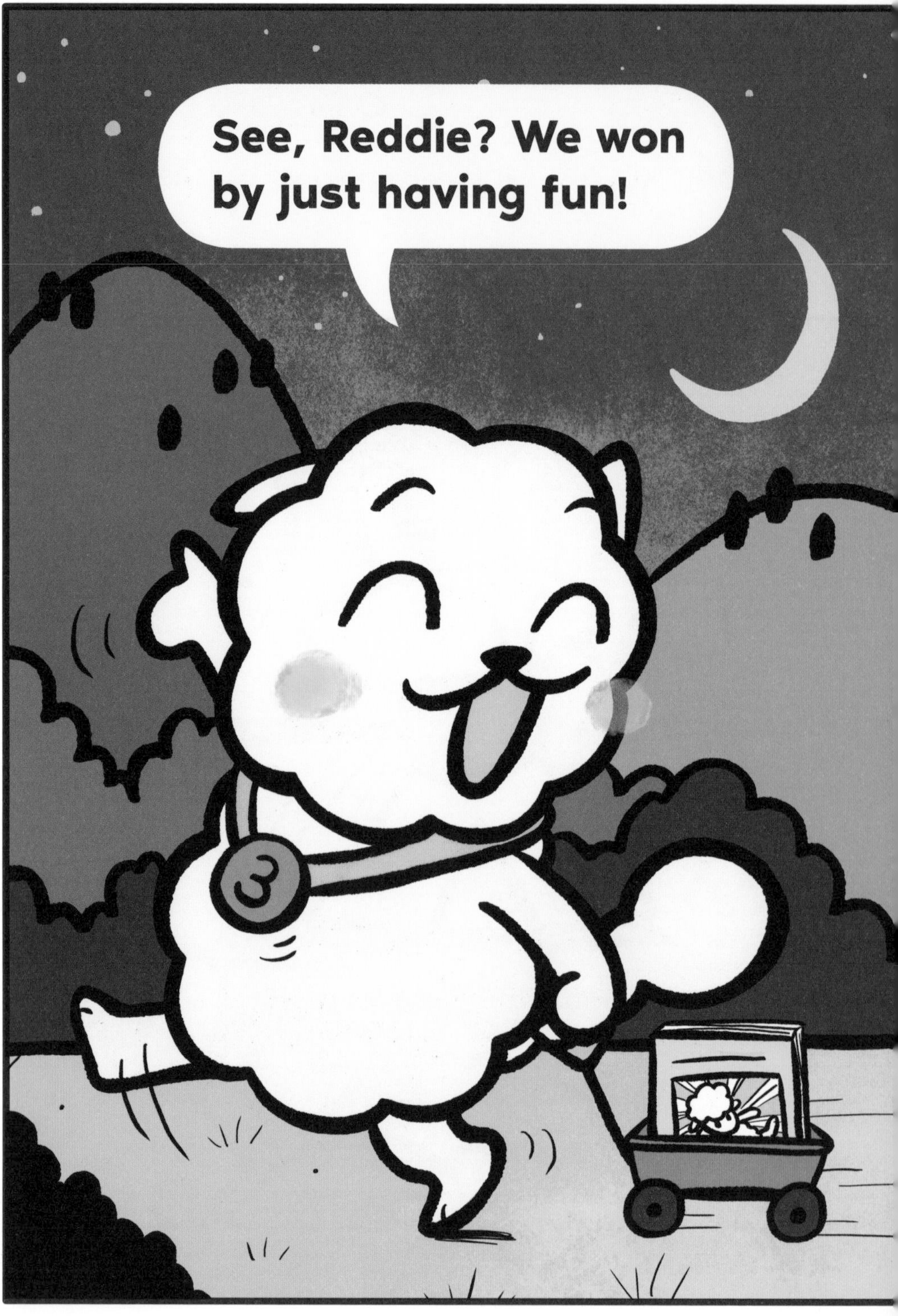
See, Reddie? We won by just having fun!

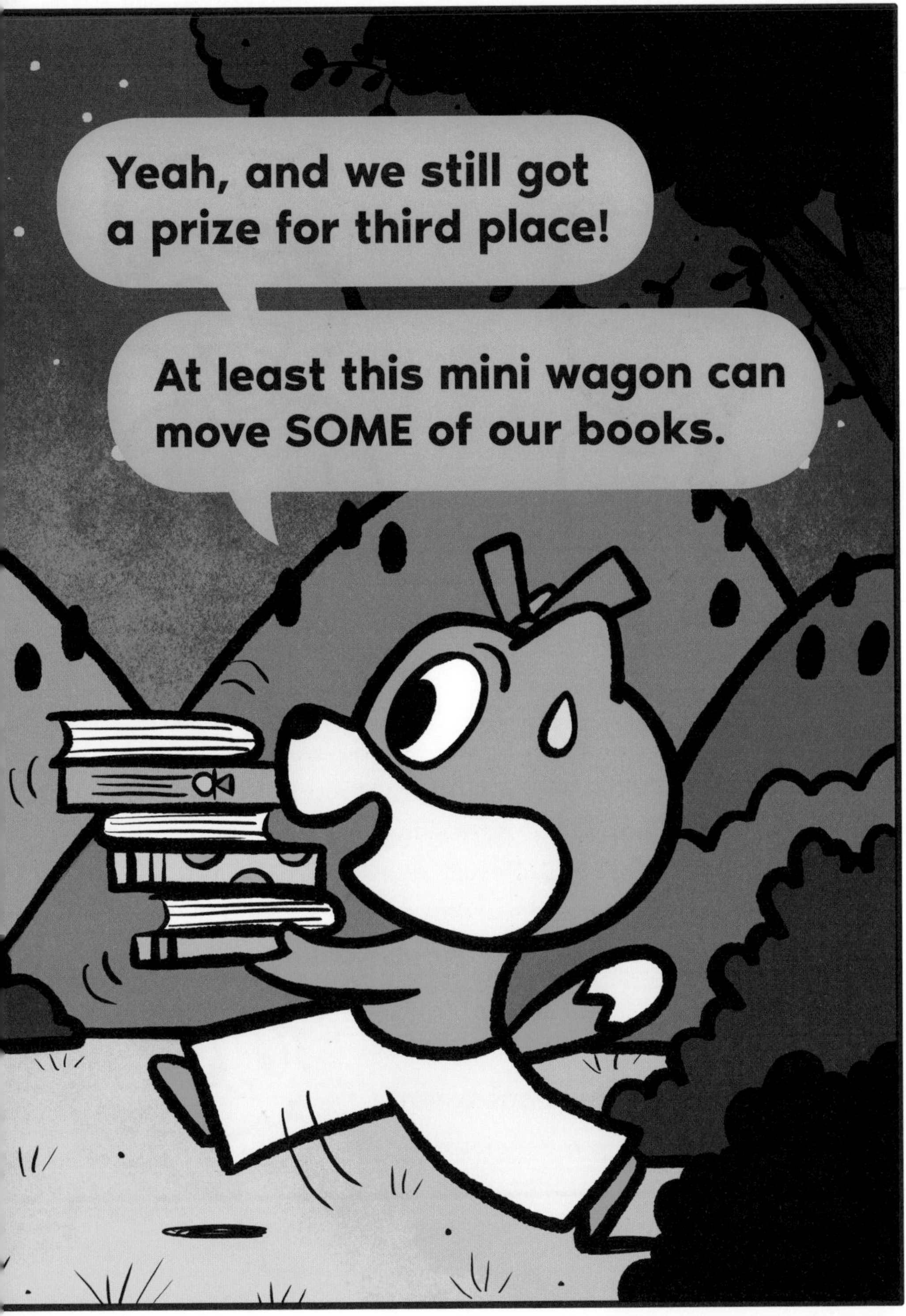
Yeah, and we still got a prize for third place!
At least this mini wagon can move SOME of our books.

MEET THE MAKERS

CANDY
draws

JAMES
writes

Candy James is a husband-and-wife creative duo originally from Hong Kong and New Zealand, but now living on a thickly forested hill in Ballarat, Australia. They are toy, graphic, and garden designers who love to make funny books for children.

What's their best talent?
Whipping up a delicious meal in the kitchen—just not while wearing skates!